Pebbles of *JADE*

Z.C. BenOHADI

Bookman
Publishing & Marketing
Providing Quality, Professional Author Services
www.bookmanmarketing.com

© Copyright 2004, Z. Christian BenOHADI

All Rights Reserved.

No part of this book may be reproduced, stored in a retrieval system, or transmitted by any means, electronic, mechanical, photocopying, recording, or otherwise, without written permission from the author.

ISBN: 1-59453-425-X

JADE… *An old fly-boy's dreams and fantasies*
(BenOHADI)

+ + +

Pebbles of Jade… *The end of hope and fantasy*
(Z.C. BenOHADI)

Dedicated to Patmos John

CONTENTS

Chapter One: BRIGADOON 1

Chapter Two: THE NISEI 13
                          SUKOSHI BRIGADE 29

Chapter Three: MEMORY OF A FOX 37
                          VOODOO 41

Chapter Four: SHADOWLANDS 51
                          JAIRUS' DAUGHTERS 57

Chapter Five: SEER SCHOOL 67
                          DREAMERS 79

Chapter Six: EXTREME DREAM 101
                          SEVENTH TENET OF FAITH.. 121

Chapter Seven: ULTIMATE THINGS 127

Chapter Eight: THE BEGINNING 191

A note from the author…
    An Irish lad named Lewis S. Clive
    Came up with the "mooreeffoc" *tribe*
    To which I humbly subscribe.
                                        Z…

99th BOMBARDMENT

LINEAGE. Organized as 99th Aero Squadron on 21 Aug 1917. Redesignated: 99th Squadron on 14 Mar 1921; 99th Observation Squadron on 25 Jan 1923. Inactivated on 31 Jul 1927. Activated on 9 Nov 1928. Redesignated: 99th Bombardment Squadron on 1 Mar 1935; 99th Bombardment Squadron (Medium) on 6 Dec 1939; 99th Bombardment Squadron (Heavy) on 20 Nov 1949; 99th Bombardment Squadron (Very Heavy) on 28 Mar 1944. Inactivated on 20 Oct 1948. Redesignated: 99th Strategic Reconnaissance Squadron (Photographic), and activated, on 1 May 1949. Redesignated: 99th Bombardment Squadron (Heavy) on 1 Apr 1950; 99th Bombardment Squadron (Medium) on 2 Oct 1950.

1

BRIGADOON

Paul said he had a story to tell and suddenly found himself surrounded by a dozen girls. They were all a little young, but beautiful! He was ushered to a chair at a small round table, a carafe of hot Sake and a small cup appeared and someone was lighting a fire in the fireplace. Beautiful piano music was coming from an unseen source and he inquired as to what it was.

"The Sake was quick… they must have a microwave," Paul thought to himself. He had called and said he was coming, but he could not believe the eagerness in their faces when he finally found this big old place between the little airport and the river. As some of them engaged him in small conversation, it seemed as if they actually *wanted* to hear his stories! "Just look at them!" he thought to himself. "There can't be more than a fifteen-year spread in their ages and they all seem to have such an eager attitude… except the younger ones who don't seem to know what is going on." He guessed the age range to be from less than two to about sixteen. They called this home of theirs "Brigadoon" and they were the "Polly

Brigade"... the phone book listed everything as *Jade West*.

The young Chinese girl serving him the Sake was genuinely apologetic, explaining she had never before served such an unusual beverage to such a distinguished Japanese guest. Not understanding their customs was making her nervous about doing it correctly. She spoke to him as if he were her grandfather, with nary a shred of apparent uneasiness.

"The music you are hearing is Chopin's *"Romance: Larghetto"* by Krystian Zimerman. I know because I put it on when we heard you were on your way and almost here," the girl said.

With no children of his own and from sixty to seventy years age difference between him and them, he could tell this was going to be fun. But, he was curious. What had they told all these little orphan-girls in Idaho about him? It was strange *enough* there should even be this Chinese orphanage in the American West. While he waited he studied the bright, smiling, giggling little round faces... and started making faces at them while twisting his goatee, which made them giggle in delight even more.

Suddenly there was the noise of running feet on the front porch and a little doll-like face, no more than seven or eight years old, poked her head through the door and shouted to the girl who had served the Sake, "Polly, here they come!"

Paul looked up and could see a small cloud of dust where a car had swung around the yard to the front of the old building they were in. Polly clapped her hands twice, quickly, and all the girls quieted down and sat as primly and properly as they knew how. They were still smiling.

Peter Benjamin walked in, saw their guest and shouted, "Paul!" They hugged for a longer than expected time. Then he said, "Paul, let me introduce you to my wife, Su-mei. The last time you two met was in San Francisco… before we were married… and so much has changed since then."

Su-mei stepped out from behind Peter and embraced Paul. Neither of them said anything. The room was silent. Then Peter continued, "After all these years, it is so good to see you again. Thank you for writing… we didn't expect you were still alive and came as soon as we got Polly's call on the cell-phone. We were with Jean-Píerre at the resort on the lake. Welcome to Jade West! We are so anxious to find out from you what happened and how you found us… and I'm sure you have some questions we can now answer. Please sit down."

Both Peter and Su-mei's eyes were wet as they sat in three ladder-back chairs around the little round table with the Sake. Su-mei whispered something to Polly and she went into the kitchen. The rest of the girls just sat, mesmerized, and in a semicircle on one side of the overly large living room called the *"great room."* Outside the big window the view suddenly dimmed, but it was still too early for the sun to set. It was just going behind West Mountain… highlighting the snow on the ridge and making the Fall colors along the riverbank grow richer and deeper as if a French *impressionist* was painting. Soon Polly appeared with a bottle of plum wine and glasses for Peter and Su-mei, referring to them as "grandfather" and "grandmother," then poured more Sake for old Paul. He bowed his head slightly while giving her an "arigato," then looked directly at his friends.

"Well, for starters" began Paul, "your friend Pete, that old *pirate* on Miyako Jima, said to say 'hi' and to come see him sometime."

"You met 'old Pete'?" both Peter and Su-mei said together. Su-mei seemed to be bouncing on her chair, more tears in her eyes and sort of short of breath. Peter stood up, walked in a circle around his chair, sat back down and took Su-mei's hands in his.

"This is too much!" Peter exclaimed. "We want to hear about him, but first we want to hear about you!"

"Not much to tell..." Paul shrugged, but was interrupted by loud chuckles from all the girls as they put their hands over their mouths. "Well, lets see... where to begin," he continued with a wrinkled smile and a twinkle in his eyes.

"It kind of hurts to remember back to when we last saw each other, so much really bad stuff has happened since then... and Su-mei, I cannot begin to imagine what you must have gone through. I heard from the *Agency* that you lost all of your immediate family and quite a few of your extended family. I am really sorry."

"It was very hard at first," Su-mei responded. "It was surreal and difficult to comprehend the magnitude of the reality. Following what happened in New York City and the global repercussions of the *War* against terrorism, it was almost overwhelming. It forced me to remember they were Christian and had the real peace they'd waited for so long. From Peter's parents in China we had learned to trust in the promises of *Shang-ti*, or *Sha-dai*... the almighty maker of everything. The sense of personal loss was tremendous, but I am okay now. Did you lose any family, Paul? I'm sorry, I don't remember hearing anything."

"No, I have been alone for many years now. However, I have recently met someone I really like... we're pretty serious. When I was visiting that old *pirate* friend of yours, Pete on Miyako-Jima. At first I thought this woman was 'sweet' on him and could not understand, because he's at least ten-years older than me. Can you imagine my curiosity? Then I found out she really *was* sweet on him... but for another reason. She's his daughter!"

"Paul, you are too old! How old are you?"

"I'm seventy-six. But she is no '*spring-chicken*' either... she's sixty-two, her husband was the local druggist and died of a heart attack shortly after the Chinese tried to start that third big war. They had several children, but they all have families in Japan and she does not want to move back there. She likes Miyako and Shimoji."

Peter turned to the children, "You remember us telling you about Shimoji-Shima and Miyako-Jima?" He quickly looked at Su-mei, then said to Paul with a puzzled look on his face, "Pete said he and his wife had no children."

"They didn't," Paul responded. "Shortly after the *'kami-sami kyosan-shugi hari-kari'*... or suicide of the communist god, as they refer to what happened to the old China... Pete's wife just went to sleep... with him and the lady from the *Salty Dog Saloon* that was working for them holding her hands. She never woke up again... just died peacefully. It was then that they let it be known this lady, Yulin, was really his daughter, illegitimately, from before he met and married his wife, Mary. He never told her... or anyone. Yulin's mother was a drug addict and died shortly after she was born. She was an orphan and as the years went by, Pete got her and Mary together. She sort of adopted Mary as her mother. Mary and Pete were both good to her, she loved them and when I went out there Pete introduced her to me."

"How is it you got to Miyako and met old Pete in the first place? How did you know anything about him?" Su-mei asked.

"After the People's Republic of China tried to 'do in' the U.S. with their off-shore nuke attacks and some assistance from North Korean missiles, I figured I better check back in with the *Agency* and see if I could help in any way. The War on Terror had caused considerable shake-up in all the intelligence agencies, so there were a lot of vacancies as disgruntled employees bailed out. There were a lot of meetings trying to figure out what happened and what to do... things were pretty chaotic... I met an agent named Mark, with the NIS, who said he knew you folks. He didn't want to tell me much, but did tell me about this guy named 'Pete' at the *Salty Dog* on Miyako-Jima out in the China Sea that might be able to answer some questions for me. There were a lot of other things they put me to work doing and it took a long time, more than several years, to come up with a way to get out there. That place is way out of the way of everything, you know!"

"We know," Peter chuckled. "That's why we escaped to that particular place for our honeymoon, which you probably didn't know."

After another sip of Sake Paul continued, "Oh. *That's* why you went out there! Well, I finally made it… spent several months getting to know the old *pirate* and learning all I could about you folks. He kept a neat little airplane over on Shimoji and we did a lot of flying together. It was an old 1946 Swift he had painted Navy Blue and it flew really well doing 'acro' in and around all the low, little puffy clouds. You're an old aviator so I can tell you all this and you'll understand. The only thing I did not like about it was when straight and level… it would *not* hold still. The rudder always wanted to 'walk' and it waddled like an old Bonanza." Paul's hands were now starting to "fly" as he spoke, almost knocking the Sake bottle off the table.

"By the way, even old Pete did not know where you folks were. Then, one day these Hawaiian gals came in to perform in the lounge, the tourists loved them, especially the Japanese, and Pete introduced me to them. I think they were called the *Ladies K*… which had nothing to do with their real names, and said they knew you folks quite well… and here I am."

"Are you working for the 'Agency'? We thought they got you a retirement." Peter asked.

"I'm still retired. At my age I have to be! However, I have volunteered a lot of my time travelling around to all the satellite operations giving briefings and answering questions because of my 'experiencial' education in China just before the '*almost*' war. The State Department picks up my expenses, but that's all. I'm cheap."

"Why all the travel? Why don't they just use you at their school?"

"The 'Anti-terrorism' school is gone, remember? There is no more 'Quantico' and they think a centralized federal school system, or seat of federal government for that matter, is too vulnerable to terrorist organizations. As you know, everything is spread out around the States now, connected only by much better-linked communications systems. Interpol has now done the same thing as the FBI. There are no more elitist federal '*experts*' now... everything is much more regional and localized. We seem to be back to our many united *States* again and everything now makes more sense and is less expensive to the taxpayers... a lot more efficient."

Looking around at the girls as he sipped a little sake, he noticed he was losing the interest of the younger ones, but knew he had to continue a little more... to wrap things up.

"As you have probably seen on the news, the giant messes along the coastal States are keeping everyone busy. They're getting cleaned up, with a lot of help from all the other States… just like ten years ago. Many things will never go back to the way they were. There was such massive coastal infrastructure destruction. As a nation we thought we had learned a lot from that attack on the World Trade Center in Manhattan, but we were still naïve regarding the inventiveness of minds inspired by evil and the resultant fear caused by the loss of true freedom. The same thing happened in Russia after the fall of communism over there. I would guess all of you learned all this in history classes." Then, kind of muttering to himself, "I'm beginning to think the Devil *is* real."

After studying his Sake awhile he looked up and continued, "The classroom situations I have been in for the last few years indicate much less emphasis is being placed on the 'politically correct' textbooks approved by the academic community these days. Much more attention is being paid to honest, not *interpreted*, American and World history. Also, much more importance is being placed on lessons from human experience than on 'approved' textbook and academic, *by-the-numbers*, credentials. However, more new textbooks are starting to come out which are historically more objectively honest and much better for the kids. Some of the old, die-hard liberals are crying that they are too old-fashioned and boring, but they don't get the 'press' they used to. It seems America has woken up from its almost deadly sleep. Even the *press* has changed… no longer quite so interested in keeping everyone arguing by aggressively stimulating debate.

BenOHADI

When old, left-over communist regimes like North Korea are desperately trying to quickly evolve so as to keep up with the world... you know something serious is happening!"

Looking up at the ceiling and kind of rolling his eyes, he smiled and said, "Sorry I got on my *soapbox* and on a *roll*... I'll try not to do that again. It's hard to catch myself and stop."

Paul looked around the room and noticed some of the younger girls *had* fallen asleep. He just could *not* go back to that old bad habit again like this. The kids wanted to hear *stories*, so he turned to Polly and asked, "What would all of you like to hear about?"

Peter interrupted, "Oh, I am sorry! How rude we are. Our girls and you have not even been introduced."

Su-mei jumped up and Polly joined her to help as they stood by each of the girls, even a couple really young ones that were sound asleep, and introduced them. Starting with the eldest seated child, Polly took their hand and they stood while Su-mei gave their Chinese and English names. Paul noticed they all had "Jade" as a middle name. When she finished the last child, Mary Jade Heaven, who had just celebrated her second birthday and was just barely walking... when she was awake, she turned to her assistant and said, "Last, but certainly not least, is our eldest daughter, 'Elizabeth Jade Star'... she was our first."

Su-mei saw the confused look on Paul's countenance, smiled and continued, "The name 'Polly' is the title of respect she is given for being the leader of the brigade which is named after Polly Bemis. She was a famous Chinese girl that had been sold in China, but survived a difficult life along *The River of No Return* in Idaho. Elizabeth was born in Taiwan, but will soon be moving to where Polly Bemis came from… the Middle Kingdom, the mainland of China, and the next eldest will become the new 'Polly' of their brigade. She has many responsibilities, including being their 'mother'… I am their 'grandmother.' You may call her Elizabeth. If you prefer to refer to her as 'oldest daughter,' then you may find it very difficult to remember the sequence of 'second, 'third, 'fourth' and so on down to 'twelfth oldest daughter.' It is up to you."

Peter chuckled and said, "You better stay with their names, Paul. It's easier. Besides, I am told things are even changing on the mainland in their culture. They still show respect, especially to their elders and those in authority, but it no longer just comes with seniority or sexual gender.

"By the way, the term 'sexual preference' will cause them to laugh. They remember with sad amusement the liberal '*agenda*' days in the U.S. and immediately will tell you that they too have 'sexual preference': the girls prefer boys… who prefer girls. Fortunately, the commitment of marriage never was out of *vogue* with the Chinese, in spite of Marxist propaganda."

"Thank you, Su-mei," Paul said. "Okay, Elizabeth, what would your brigade like to hear?"

She stood and walked in front of all the others and faced him with her hands folded in front of her. She bowed and said, "The Polly Brigade of Brigadoon

BenOHADI

would be honored to hear all of your life's story so it can be part of the history of our lives we pass on to our families some day. Please begin at the beginning."

Paul had stood up when she bowed to him. He looked at the other girls and said, "You are asking for a lot. Do you have that much time? Is there anything in particular you would like to hear first before I begin such a task?"

The little one he had seen poking her head in the door earlier piped up and said, "Tell us about Pirate Pete!" Polly closed her eyes and the little urchin put her hands in front of her mouth. Everyone giggled.

"I will," Paul laughed. "Why don't we just wait until we get to him. He's fun. He has had a lot of adventure I know you will enjoy. Too bad you cannot get *him* here." He looked at Peter and Su-mei.

Su-mei responded, "Maybe someday we will. Paul, you may stay with us as long as you like and we look forward to introducing you to the congregation of Christians we worship with on Sunday mornings. We have plenty of time and consider this part of the girls' education." Then she looked at the girls and said, "Major Uhara will speak *to* you and *with* you for three hours every evening after dinner." She looked at Paul and asked, "Do you feel up to it?"

"Yes, I look forward to it...for a few weeks only. Then I promised Yulin I would be back."

2

THE NISEI

"To begin with," Paul began, "after the '*almost*' war when I started working with the *Agency* again, the NIS and FBI also reviewed my case and decided I had been short-changed. My almost-forty years of 'E & E' (escape and evasion) in the Peoples Republic of China were honorable and I was exonerated regarding being there in the first place. The OSI (Office of Special Intelligence) had already begun paperwork on me to serve as an agent before all this happened. I brought back much cultural information which they would have had a hard time obtaining and had I stayed in the military I could have been at least a Lieutenant Colonel upon retirement... so they gave me a *backdated* promotion. Now you can call me 'Colonel' Uhara... but please don't!"

Paul chuckled, took another sip and continued. "I just feel very fortunate. They even gave me quite a little back pay which has paid for the personal flights I've taken recently."

After tossing down the rest, "My parents grew up together as friends in the little village of Fusa. Shortly after they were married my father found a good job in

Shinjuku, then Shinagawa working on railroad communications systems. They sensed Japan was gearing up militarily and when openings were announced for some new work on communications systems in Hawaii, they applied and were moved from the island of Honshu to the island of Oahu.

"I was born in Honolulu ten years before 'Pearl Harbor' and started school there. By then my parents had many friends and neighbors that were Chinese, because of Hawaii being such an ethnic *melting pot*. They did not like what they were hearing regarding what their Emperor Hirohito and the Imperial Army were doing in China and began to suspect why their transfer to this job had been so easy... deciding they would rather become American citizens than civilian spies. This was possible because the Hawaiian Islands were a Trust Territory of the United States. By then I spoke more dialects of Chinese than any Japanese or English. My parents actually became American citizens before the Japanese Imperial Air Force attacked the American Navy, but it made no difference. They were shipped to an internment camp in California anyway as a precaution against any *fifth column* activities based on blood-loyalty. It was there, with so many others of my race, where I learned most of my Japanese, including many different dialects."

Paul looked a little uncomfortable, but continued, "After the war, we were shipped back to Honolulu and my parents immediately moved me to a little village on the windward side of Oahu named Waimanalo. They wanted to move out of the city and into the country for safety reasons. Only after they moved and settled in there did they find out one of their relatives had preceded them. He was the number two man of an Imperial Navy two-man, or midget submarine (MA-19) that had become stuck in their beach on the 8th of December 1941and had the distinction of *almost* being the first Japanese prisoner after the attack on Pearl Harbor. He drowned trying to escape. His captain was an Ensign Kazuo Sakamaki and I understand he might still be alive in Florida somewhere. He must be very old. Pictures taken at the time are easily identified because of Rabbit Island in the background."

While he had been talking, Polly had heated a little more Sake and poured it for him. "I was a typical kid and did a lot of kid stuff, but never got into any real trouble with the law. In those days everyone remembered how opium had made China weak and so drugs were not a problem… none of us wanted to deliberately give in to that kind of self-destructive weakness. We drank a lot of beer, but the times we got 'drunk' were more psychological than real. I surfed and fished in the ocean a lot. To this day, the Waimanalo-Bellows Beach is my favorite place in the world, except now there are just too many 'welfare' people that live in tents and kind of ruin the atmosphere for the working families.

"Upon graduation from Kailua High School I attended the University of Hawaii and became an Air Force ROTC cadet. The university is not far from Waikiki, the world-famous beach where all the tourists went, so that became a favorite hangout when some of my beer-drinking buddies and I were looking for a little action. In those days, there were not so many hotels on the beach and we just rode the Number 4 Bus down to the Royal Hawaiian Hotel and head for the bar on the beach... to start looking for the beauties on the sand. We soon discovered there was a much less expensive way to begin our expedition down the beach... the Barefoot at the Fort DeRussy Officers Club. Since we had Air Force ROTC Cadet ID cards, they let us in. Not only were the beers cheaper than at the ritzy, pink hotel, but we also met military people who could answer a lot of questions. We were pleasantly surprised to find none were the *'war-mongers'* we had been told they would be from so many of our college professors. Nobody wanted a World War Three. Soon we were also meeting and drinking with combat-ready pilots that were on R&R (rest and recuperation). Those silver wings twinkled of very appealing adventure which we would talk endlessly about as we made our way down to the far end of Waikiki. The Queens Surf Hotel always had a Tahitian Dance show in the evening, which we did not want to miss. It wasn't as culturally beautiful as a Hula show, but was a lot more titillating. Remember, we were still young college boys... who drank too much!

"My double-majors at the university were Photojournalism and International Affairs, but I met all the qualifications and the Air Force gave me a pilot slot upon receiving my ROTC commission. After my graduation they sent me to USAF Undergraduate Pilot

Training… and also seemed intensely interested in my Asian language skills. Things were looking good.

"Officers and cadets did not go to 'Basic Training' as Enlisted personnel did. We did pretty much the same thing at Lackland AFB in Texas as regular enlisted troops did, but it was called 'Pre-Flight Training'. When that phase was over, I did not have enough time to visit home, so I spent a week getting to know San Antonio and the Alamo. I kind of liked the place and today they have fixed up everything I thought was needed at the time. I even went out with a young girl named Maria Elena de la Fuente from Mexico City, who was attending Incarnate Word College, a Roman Catholic girls boarding school. Of course, she was never allowed to go out alone, so they were always 'double-dates', or at chaperoned parties. I'll bet she probably still talks about the Jap-American lieutenant she once dated."

Paul stood up. He wanted to be able to use his hands as he talked about airplanes. "The next assignment was to Bartow Air Base in Florida where we started training in Air Force T-34 aircraft. Beechcraft's name for them was the 'Mentor'. I was finally a pilot, even if only a student. It was challenging, but really satisfying, especially after I soloed, and could fly around in the puffy-clouded skies of southern Florida with the sliding canopy open. We were allowed to do everything we had learned: some acrobatics, including spins, and practice 'forced landings' on just about any open field we could find. It was fun trying to 'bomb' cows with the helmet-bag full of oranges we sometimes carried (secretly) for that purpose. In case you are worried about the cows... I am reasonably positive we never hit any." Some of the girls smiled a little. One of the little ones was pretending to drop oranges out the side of an airplane and her little stool slipped, dropping her on the floor. They all laughed.

To prevent interfering with the T-37 jet-training operation that would come next, we often flew out of the auxiliary Gilbert Field with our T-34s. The one thing we were not to do out there was go near a privately owned B-25 some guy was fixing up... supposedly for civilian use. We were told the CIA was across the street in a motel watching it, to make sure it was not taken to Cuba. No one wanted a repeat of the recent "Bay of Pigs" fiasco. I thought at the time I was as close to the mysterious CIA as I would ever be."

After coughing with a little smile, "Once I did fly to Tampa and back solo. (It really is remarkable they trusted us so, but it did teach us responsibility.) I even *shot,* that is *did,* a *'missed approach'* at McDill AFB from a visual pattern. The tower operators knew I was a student and were very helpful. Then I did something stupid. On the way back I leaned out of the cockpit just a little to look at something on the ground and the wind caught my ball-cap. Losing it was not so bad, but it pulled my headset off! (We did not yet wear helmets.) Now I was in big trouble! I figured I could probably get away with losing the headset and its attached boom-microphone if it were not that I would now *not* be able to communicate with anyone! My mind raced as I tried

Pebbles of JADE

to dream up some reasonable story. It was impossible. I pulled the canopy closed and tried to think as I navigated home. Even landing somewhere else first would not explain things. I would have to make a 'radio-out' landing and when they found out why... I was finished. Then I noticed something pulling on my neck. It was the headset cord! It was tight! When I twisted around a little I could see the cord pulling down over the back-seat panel just past where it connected to the aircraft cord. It had gone into the back cockpit over the instrument panel and was still in the airplane! Now, I knew the T-34 had oil and fuel pumps allowing for inverted flight of limited duration, so I went into about a thirty-degree climb, rolled the bird over, and pushed the 'stick' forward until the dust was coming off the floor. Then I pulled back on the throttle and decelerated while almost holding altitude. Sure enough, the headset fell to the canopy and slid forward along the top of the canopy until I could grab the cord past the connection... so it would not come loose. I had it! The hardest thing was recovering the airplane to straight and level while struggling to get all of the dirt and junk out of my eyes. I was so excited and just knew that somewhere during those moments of panic I must have prayed a little, because it was then I started remembering to pray more often... and I started going to Chapel. Believe me, considering how badly I wanted to make it through that program, when I landed I had a hard time explaining why I was so happy after just another routine, scheduled *solo* flight. They mistook my *relief* for happiness... and I couldn't even tell my story to anyone! At sometime during my military academic training I learned to *never* volunteer information."

Paul's mind drifted a little as he thought back to that almost boyhood, confidence-building ecstasy.

"Next came the T-37. What a neat little airplane that was! It was a side-by-side, two-seater, two-engine, fully aerobatic, fuel efficient little trainer. It was a sports car, a jet Ferrari! I really loved it and could never understand why Cessna never made a civilian version of it. However, it did use a lot of runway and the high-pitched, screaming little engines earned the nickname: 'Tweety-bird'. We wore helmets not only to muffle the sound and survive ejections (it had ejection seats), but also to be able to use oxygen masks... the cockpit was non-pressurized and the little trainer could fly quite high. Curiously, our instructor pilots were *civilians* who worked under contract for the Servair Corporation. They were all retired military pilots from before the jet-age and must have really loved their jobs! I only heard of one 'loss' that occurred just before we got there.

"There was an all girls' college for rich kids from the Northeast on a lake nearby. A student pilot from Bartow had been dating one of them and was 'buzzing' their beach. He tried to do an aileron-roll, but was too low and caught a wingtip on the water. The little bird just totally disintegrated. There was not much left of him. We all know that lust can cause people to do dumb things... and he must have been thinking with his other head as he tried to impress her. Their school became temporarily *Off Limits* to us and we felt cheated."

"Polly" (Elizabeth) let out a squeal. Then put her hands to her mouth and looked around, knowing she might have to explain some things to the younger ones.

"Bartow Air Base (Not a full blown Air Force Base) was near the community of Winter Haven and Cyprus Gardens... a great place to go when off-duty. All the lakes in the area were connected with canals, so we could even 'boat' over there with the little *outboards* from our *rec*-department. They had a great 'water-show' for the tourists, and most importantly, they hired very attractive young girls to just sit around in the flower gardens and look pretty for pictures. Most of the officers from the base were married, so it was the cadets who had the club on base with all the action. There was even a beautiful Aviation Cadet logo artistically fashioned into the parquet dance floor. I found that on almost any given weekend night at the Cadet Club, if I would (try to) disguise myself in civilian clothes, there would always be two or three of those girls there... without dates and presumably available. Most of the other girls there would be from Florida Southern University in Lakeland. They and their parents all wanted them to latch onto one of those single flying cadets, who would soon have their silver wings and gold officer bars. The Club had a full-blown swimming pool with diving boards... and flight-suit parties were the rage. Zippers that exposed cleavage were always kept coming down as the evenings wore

BenOHADI

on… and it was evident there was rarely much under those flight suits they'd borrowed."

Elizabeth stood up and walked behind the other girls. Was she blushing? Paul knew he was going too far. His memories of those really exciting, youthful years were coming back too strongly and he knew he'd better cool it a little. He was afraid to continue, but he glanced up at Su-mei. She smiled, caught his eyes and said, "It's okay, Paul. They need to learn how young guys *think*. It helps them prepare," she chuckled.

So he went on. "Well, what was called 'Primary Flight Training' at Bartow Air Base was exhilarating and enjoyable. When we flew our solo training missions we could either truly fly solo with an empty right seat, or we could take one of our class-mates along as a safety pilot…to help 'clear' us on the right side of the airplane when necessary in turns. Our buddy in the right seat could even log 'copilot' time in his logbook. It was fun, but do not get me wrong, it was also really hard academically and physically. Guys were regularly 'washing out' either by failing the various check-rides, or just by not keeping up with things. Less than twenty percent of the Aviation Cadets made it all the way through to getting their *wings*. The officers did better because so many were already eliminated in the AFROTC pilot selection process… and already having a college degree, there was another career waiting for them if they did not feel particularly committed to the Air Force. They approached all the training from a much more relaxed attitude." Polly had composed herself and sat back down.

"We were not allowed cars during 'Preflight Training' at Lackland. But when that phase of training was finished and after a brief visit back home, I flew back and drove mine to 'Primary Training' at Bartow. It was an all-white, 1954 Oldsmobile 98 Starfire convertible... the perfect car for down there, I thought. Red and white leather, power everything, 'wonderbar' (signal seeking AM) radio, power top, good sounding V-8. I had a really good road construction job during my years at UH, scholarships, AFROTC scholarship and monthly stipend not only got me through the college debt-free, but also allowed me to save enough to buy that car before I left San Antonio. I desperately wanted to buy a Dual Ghia convertible that was also for sale down there, but it cost *way* too much. Once I even chased down a Chrysler 300 convertible I had seen... with a manual transmission, but the guy would not even talk about selling it. The Olds worked out great and I saw a lot of the U. S with the top down. The drive back from Florida, up through the Smokey Mountains and cross-country back to Texas for 'Basic Flight Training' at Reese AFB, just outside of Lubbock was a great education in *Americana*. I have always loved driving down small country highways and through small towns, especially when the weather was nice and I had a *"rag top"*... day *or* night. Have any of you girls had any opportunity to explore America much?"

Silence.

"You will, soon enough. The heartland of the South, the Mid-West and some of the Western areas probably most closely resemble early America... as long as you stay away from the cities, stadiums, airports and freeways, where most of the terrorism has occurred. You will discover that a city is a city is a city. In a way they are all pretty much the same in that they provide continuous distraction from what I would call the 'real life' that involves closer involvement with nature. The coasts, east and west, are slowly recovering and coming back to life after those horrible nuclear tides... and New York City had that 'double whammy'. They will never be the same, especially because of the tremendous loss of life. As you know, first the Middle-Eastern terrorists hit the World Trade Center and the Pentagon, then just as we were making progress eliminating their 'cells' in other countries and ours, ethno-centric Chinese terrorists hit the coastal cities. So many buildings were either destroyed or ruined that the big problem has been what to do with the rubble. Getting electrical power back into those areas safely is an on-going problem. Some of the destroyed businesses are relocating inland, but many are just shutting down and others are replacing them. At the moment, with so much disruption of monopolistic industry, there are many new entrepreneurial opportunities. In some ways it is like America starting all over again, only with a 'high-tech' starting point. Unfortunately, finding investors is still difficult."

Paul sat back down... he knew he'd been on a rambling-*roll*. "Let me just wrap up my story about how I got flying in the military in the first place. Then before I continue it would be good if I could learn a little about some of you and what your interests are."

Su-mei poured a little Sake for Paul and plum wine for Peter. Paul savored it for a moment, thinking he'd better slow down... then continued, "Back in my days they were still using the old T-Birds for training. The Lockheed T-33 was a good, tough old bird. Sort of the 'Gooney Bird' of the jet-trainer era. For you kids that don't know a whole lot about airplanes, the C-47, or DC-3 in the civilian world, was called the 'Gooney Bird' because it could survive so many really rough landings. You will probably have to watch the real Gooney Birds on Wake Island, as I once did, to understand what I am talking about. C-47s are still flying! That old tail-dragger was the first of the high production, pressurized, long-distance passenger and cargo airplanes."

Seeing the kids were looking a little bored, probably from a lack of aviation-history comprehension, a little panic set in. "Anyway, the T-Bird did not have nose-wheel steering, only differential braking... and it used a lot of runway to get off the ground... but it was a good trainer for going on into fighters and jet bombers. However, there were frequent transient aircraft coming through our base... and even air-shows that exposed me to a real variety of airplanes. I was getting a good idea of what I wanted to fly when I got my *wings.* I also knew I did not want to get married and be 'tied down' right away. I wanted some adventuresome assignments to remote areas I knew would not be good for married life... that could come later."

Trying to look sad... "My Olds Starfire *bit-the-dust* before I completed training, so I traded it in on an Alfa

BenOHADI

Romeo 1300 Guilietta Veloce Spyder at Fawcett Motors in Lubbock. This sophisticated little Italian sports car turned out to be a wonderful, and very fast, set of wheels. Bunches of us would often head south, through the Texas cap-rock areas, to Mexico. A gaggle of little cars with their tops down driven by 'wannabe' pilots was probably dangerous, but so much fun! The only frustration was this little MG that could always outrun us... turned out it was a *'twin-cam'* version."

Now frowning... "The 'girl' situation was a little different. The atmosphere at Texas Tech, in Lubbock, was sort of anti-military... and this was even long before Vietnam. The teachers and the students pretty much stuck their noses up at us. But the nurses' colleges in the area were a different story altogether! They seemed to be very practical minded and treated us like royalty! There were many good parties, many spent a lot of time at the Reese AFB Cadet Club on base, and we were invited to many great 'outings' that included swimming, picnics, and horseback riding. We really appreciated them... but I did not want to get serious with anyone yet. Some of my friends did end up with happy marriages, but I was really getting focused on what I wanted to do in the Air Force about that time."

Smiling... "When I finally graduated, my parents flew in and my mother pinned my newly earned wings on me, my father took pictures... then he proudly pinned the brass bars of a Second Lieutenant on me. One of the nurses I knew really 'buttered up' to Mama, who could not figure out why I would not want to marry such a nice, pretty (but a little too plump), well-mannered and educated young lady. It was hard to explain. My mind was still on just meeting another solo T-Bird up over Dragon Lake or buzzing the Roaring Springs swimming pool on the way to Muleshu and doing some formation buzzing or 'dog-fighting'. The little boy was still in me, only now I would have bigger, more powerful and faster toys to play with... expensive government equipment at government expense! (So much for envying *heavy-equipment* operators!) Plus, I looked forward to the responsibility of doing important things for the U.S. in the world. I guess you might say that by then I was a 'playboy-patriot'."

He was relieved to see the girls paying attention again. "We received our 'Advanced Pilot Training' assignments, but before we could go to them, those with combat aircraft assignments had to go to 'Survival Training School' at Stead AFB outside of Reno in the Sierra Mountain Range of Nevada. That not only included snow, mountains and woods, but also *enemy* escape and evasion. It was good and would pay off later... I'll come to that... maybe, if I shorten this a little."

Not wanting this to be a *shaggy-dog story* and wanting to *rush* a little... "After *Stead*, I went to Shaw AFB for McDonnell Aircraft-built F-101 Voodoo School. That was a dream come true. The most powerful, elegant, twin-engine, afterburnered, single-seat fighter I could imagine ever wanting to fly. It could do everything... even with an engine failure. It had just set a transcontinental speed record averaging over a thousand miles an hour, round-trip, from coast to coast. When I finished checking out in that beautiful 'bird' some of my buddies started flying them on (what was called) 'sight-seeing' trips over Cuba. Intelligence said the Soviet Union was putting in medium-range missiles and they wanted some high-speed, low altitude, sharp-resolution pictures."

Folding his hands on the table... "For my first 'combat-ready' assignment they sent me the other direction to do some 'sight-seeing' in Southeast Asia, which I'll tell you about after I have listened to you a little. French Indo-China had been making the news for a long time."

Su-mei nodded to Polly who told all the girls to take a ten-minute break, get some refreshments in the kitchen and then come back. Paul noticed that certain of the older girls took charge of some of the very young ones. Su-mei took care of little Anna Jade. The only noisy chattering was in the kitchen. Peter showed Paul where the guest bathroom was downstairs and said he would give him a tour of the whole place after the children had gone to bed. Paul was feeling a little animated. He did not know if it was finally visiting with Peter and Su-mei after all that had happened, the presence of so many interested young people, the Sake, or the memories he had not dwelled on for so many years... nobody ever wanted to hear about his memories. It felt good. He felt young again.

SUKOSHI BRIGADE

"You are girls, not boys," Paul began. "I know you think differently than I did. I wanted to work with mechanical things that could be an extension of myself as a human and would make me sort of *superhuman*. I also had a desire for adventure and excitement. I suspect even American born girls think a little differently... I think it is just a *girl-thing*. Am I right? You're being raised in America, how do you think? What would you like to be doing when you grow up? Most of you were born in Taiwan, do you think you *think* differently than girls born over here?"

Silence. The older girls just looked at each other and raised their eyebrows. The junior-high aged ones put their hands to their mouths and giggled silently. The really young ones did not seem to have any idea of what he was talking about...in fact, they looked like they were ready for bed. Evidently Su-mei thought so too and talked to Elizabeth. Soon an announcement was made that they would have their evening dinner differently tonight... they would eat in shifts. Group three (the youngest) would eat first, in about fifteen minutes and would then be excused to their rooms. 'Polly' signaled and the four oldest girls followed her into the kitchen to start preparing something for them. Paul was left to talk to seven girls aged two to twelve.

Immediately, as soon as the older girls left the room, the little round-faced 'urchin' who had spoken through the door earlier, stood and seemed to take charge. "I am Anna Jade Bright. I am twelve and in the seventh grade in school this year." Paul was surprised... he had thought her much younger. She continued, "In most ways we are like all our girlfriends at school who were born in America... except for one born in China. But in one way we seem to be very different and seem to continually disappoint our women teachers. We want to learn to do things we are interested in, but mostly, we want to get married and raise families that include boys *and* girls with husbands who have good jobs. Grandmother Benjamin says that may be because we missed out on that in our lives. Is that true? We have been told you lived a long time in, what they call here, Mainland China. We want to be 'normal' Chinese. Are we normal?"

"Wow!" Paul thought to himself. "She is one smart, articulate little girl. I'll bet she could put many of her teachers to shame with *her* ability to *think*. I'm not sure how to begin." He began by saying he would answer all of their questions, but was this a good question for him to begin with. They all nodded that it was. Then he asked them if he could ask them questions about themselves. Again they all nodded.

"Yes, of course you are 'normal'... especially now. Remember, in America no one is *normal*, even by international standards. That is what makes them 'normal Americans.' Does that make sense?" Everyone looked confused.

"Good. You are normal Americans. However, I suspect you're more interested in being normal *Chinese*.

"When the CCP, the Chinese Communist Party, was in charge the *Republic* was considered 'god' and the family unit was kind of looked down upon because it distracted their *proper* loyalty... where ideology was god. The older generations, especially in the countryside, knew there was something wrong with that and now they are the ones that have mostly survived their own confused and twisted ethno-centrism. So... you are 'normal' today.

America may still be behind a little and still be enamored by some of Carl Marx's teachings, even though the rest of the world has discovered it is against different forms of lust and greed in all of human nature and does not work well for long. Even babies are greedy!"

Looking around at them all, "Let me hear from the rest of you. What do you like? What excites you? What can you not get enough of? What do you want more than anything?"

Surprisingly, one little girl in the front row raised her hand and when Paul pointed to her she stood and said, "My name is Sai Jade Gold. I am not from Taiwan. I am from Soochow and was sold to some tourists as a baby. They were very good to me and brought me here to be raised by Grandfather and Grandmother. We are studying about slavery in school and about how it was different in other countries throughout history than it was here in America. In other countries it was because of war and the capturing of people as *property*. In America it was racial, but only after they were captured by people of their own race on their own African continent during various tribal wars in different countries and sold to outside traders. Was there any slavery in China when you lived there? Grandfather and Grandmother said you lived there a long time. Did our people ever have slaves? Why did you live there?"

Paul thought a moment, then answered "Let me hold off on your second question for a while, but as to slavery… it was different, but yes there was. No one recognized it because it was normal. In the early 'Dynasty' years they were enslaved by the feudal *Warlords,* but had some personal freedom… just as in Europe. When Mao started the 'Peoples Republic' they were enslaved by his *Communist Party.* Then everyone was a slave. They were *owned* and really had no more personal freedom than blacks did in the American 'south' a hundred years ago. That was what President Lincoln did not want to see legalized across this new nation. One difference in China was that the people in charge kept changing because of political and ideological competition. But, tell me about you. What do you like… and want in life?"

The little girl had been about to sit back down, but Lin took her arm and made her continue standing. She was sharp and Paul knew she could look inside herself. He just looked at her and waited.

"I want a life of adventure, too… but not by myself. I would like the protection of a husband who is smart and strong. I would be his partner, his teammate. Together, we would be stronger than just 'two'! I would like us to travel and study other cultures and the mistakes they have made. The Middle Kingdom has made many mistakes and when I grow up I would like to help fix things with my husband and family. My parents did not want me, but wanted money instead. That kind of thinking should not continue. America has an established reputation of having respect for *all* unique human life, male *or* female, conveniently wanted or not, and they do *not* sell their children… even though they legally killed them for many years. That is how I hope our people in the *New Old China* will become." She sat down.

Again Paul thought "wow!" These kids are *thinkers!* Another hand went up. The little girl *couldn't* be more than five!

"My name is Lili Jade Green and I want to be a pirate's wife. Please tell us about Pirate Pete!"

"Well, he wasn't *really* a pirate," Paul laughed. "He just had that kind of personality and it sort of just became the way I liked to think about him because of his lifestyle. Remember, he was sort of in the tourist business. I liked thinking of him as sort of a *retired* modern-day pirate. In fact, his daughter Yulin and I have been considering putting up a sign on the beach in front of the Heartbreaker Hotel that labels it 'Pirate Pete's Parade,' because he loves sitting on the balcony and watching the tourist girls in their bikinis. She calls him her 'dirty old man'… lovingly, as a daughter of course.

"Today, if you want to be a pirate's wife, you will have to move to the 'straits' south of Thailand or find an old *character* like Pete. If they are young, acting like him, they are probably just lazy bums. Be careful! It is almost impossible to *change* a bum once you have married him, regardless of how talented or *pretty* they may be... so just avoid that potentially unhappy marriage in the first place. You are too pretty to marry a bum... regardless of how 'pretty' he is! And whatever you do, regardless of what your friends say, don't ever give him a married man's *privileges* without his *commitment* as your husband. History has proven that does *not* work. In *Old* China, men thought it their 'right' to hit and beat their wives. In old *Communist* China, the government thought it their 'right' to hit and beat people into submission. Don't marry a man who *hits*."

A couple of the older girls came out of the kitchen, which jogged Paul's memory of something Bright Jade Anna had said, which he wanted to ask about before he forgot. He looked at the little girl and asked, "Bright Jade, is that your name? What did you mean when you mentioned you had a schoolmate who was born in China? Were not all of you born in China?"

She stood up, came to "attention" it looked like and said, "You have my name backwards... it is Anna. Anna Jade Bright in Chinese. Yes, we were all born in China. However, one of our friends at school is also Chinese. She was adopted by a family in town that is still raising her as their own child. She spends a lot of time out here with us doing everything, but she does have her own home."

"Do you consider her part of the "Polly Brigade" or "Brigadoon"?

Pebbles of JADE

"Yes and no. We do consider her part of the *Brigade* because she learns with us… including the karate lessons… and has been helpful to all of us, but she is not part of Brigadoon because she does not live here."

"How has she helped you, and what is her name?"

"She has helped us, Uhara-san, by teaching us *movie-star* karate. Her name is Elona Li Zimmermann."

"Zimmermann?"

"She was adopted by a German-American family we think moved here from Israel. They only say it is important for everyone, even Semites, to escape anti-Messianic influence. They always seem very busy and no one has been able to learn much about them personally."

"What does she talk about at the table with the girls?"

"She's never stayed for a meal that I can remember… and she just says her parents are retired, but never from *what*."

This is too much, Paul thought to himself.

"By 'movie-star karate' I mean it seems her idol is Lucy Liu… and she has been copying all her karate moves. Although, come to think of it, I've never heard her mention the actress by name. When Grandmother is teaching us, she sometimes calls on her to help make the moves look better for when we see some river-rafter taking movies… which has happened quite often. We've even made some special news programs… and once we were used as *extras* in the background of a

BenOHADI

Hollywood movie that was done on location across the lake at the Tamarack Resort. If you're interested, the *script* for it is over on the piano. Its entitled *'Light In Darkness'* from something written by a guy named Sergei Fudel... and, I'm told, Mel Gibson might be interested."

"Oh."

Just as Elizabeth came back into the *Great Room* to get the little ones for their supper, Anna Jade exclaimed quickly "We really *do* want to hear about Pirate Pete!" then sat down as 'Polly' took charge again and signaled the youngest group into the kitchen.

3

MEMORY OF A FOX
(Kioku mundan de Kitsune)

Elizabeth and two of the older girls came back in the room and two remained with the five littlest ones in the kitchen.

"Polly" resumed her position of authority and began, "Colonel Uhara, until all of 'group one' is together, perhaps you could answer and tell us a little more about the man our grandparents always respectfully refer to as 'old Pete'… whom Jade Bright now calls 'Pirate Pete'."

"Sure," said Paul. "But first, please don't call me Colonel. Back in my military days my ego would have loved it, but that was so long ago and my life has moved on so much since then that it makes me uncomfortable… I don't want to need to be made to feel important any more."

"Excuse me, sir," Elizabeth jumped in, her feet together and her hands behind her back. "What would you prefer we call you? We really do feel you are part of our family."

"How about just Uhara-san. That would be about right for a friend of the family and culturally correct for me at the same time. Would that be okay?"

"Yes, thank you Uhara-san." She looked at them all and they all nodded.

"Well, to begin with, old Pete is in good health and doing fine." He held up a cup of Sake and Peter and Su-mei toasted his continuing health. "In fact, with his widowed daughter now openly at his side, he seems to be growing younger. Of course he misses Mary and even though I never met her, he continually speaks of her with very fond memories. He also has very fond memories of the short time you folks spent with him and has appreciated that you have kept in touch with him… even though you never gave him your address. To this day he does not know how closely connected you two were with the 'intelligence' community… but he still has his suspicions. He just knows you folks were somehow involved and that you were on the right side. He obviously trusted you from the beginning or he would not have shown you the stuff he did. You remember… the stuff he'd accumulated from the hotel's rooms and their wastebaskets. He thinks it may have helped somehow. He didn't know anything about me, so I only explained that Peter and I were old flying buddies in the same jet bomber squadron during the *Cold War*. That was about all I could tell him. He does not know of my time in China and I couldn't even tell him how we got back together again. He and Yulin would really like for you to come and visit sometime, even though she never actually met you. Evidently you did once visit her husband at his pharmacy and caused quite a stir."

"Oh! He was the pharmacist we visited?" Su-mei exclaimed.

"Now I see the connection," said Peter as he poured *his* "Jade" a little more wine. "Remember him talking to her on the phone in Japanese when we told him what had happened?"

"Yes! This is amazing," she sort of squealed in a high voice. Continuing in a deep voice, "Oh, it is bringing back memories with such a mixture of emotions! I wasn't ready for this." Her eyes were wet and Peter put his arms around her. "I'll be okay," she said. Then looking at Paul she asked, "Are you two 'serious'?"

"She doesn't think so yet. I think we easily could be. I never thought that would happen. She looks a lot different, but has a personality similar to my wife of many years back in China. It's a little spooky. You ever had that feeling of *de-ja-vu*?"

"We can talk about that later... Paul," asked Peter, "you never told us what happened to your wife... why she died. Is it alright to ask?"

"Yeah. I never found out for sure. Every once in a while her employers at the freight yard would schedule their employees for physical examinations, which included inoculations. They said they did not want their employees getting sick and not being able to work. I began to notice some of the non-Chinese would sometimes get very sick and did not come back to work. I asked her about that and she thought it had something to do with certain 'shots' only the non-Chinese might be getting. They were often told non-Chinese were not as healthy and required more medication to keep them alive. Two days after going in for her last physical exam she went into a coma and died suddenly. It was devastating! I never could find out why and I was afraid to ask too many questions. One nurse once just said 'the foreign blood was not as strong'. The company took care of her official funeral ceremony and I never learned anything. The little 'Three-Self' congregation we worshipped with had a Christian service for her, but it had to be kept quiet. Yulin said you folks might have some information that, evidently, you had her husband get for you. Do you know something?"

"Paul..." Peter started, but Su-mei interrupted.

"We think the Chinese were doing a lot of experimenting with different forms of biological weapon and delivery systems. It is possible your wife was a victim of some of their mass experiments."

Elizabeth stood up and waited her turn, then asked, "Uhara-san, would you please continue the story you started earlier. We would like to learn more of Pirate Pete, but it can wait." She looked at Jade Bright, then sat down.

"Let's see, where were we?"

"Southeast Asia," Jade Bright volunteered.

"Oh, yeah. It was my first 'Combat Tour'...

VOODOO

"My first assignment in TAC, the Tactical Air Command, was a job connected with PACAF, the Pacific Air Command. What we first learned about back in high school as 'French Indochina' had been divided into several autonomous nations that were involved in SEATO, the South East Asia Treaty Organization. It was to function like NATO, the North Atlantic Treaty Organization did in Europe... where numerous countries in a region agreed to band together while defending small governments that found themselves besieged by power-hungry and expansionist, ideological greed.

"They sent six of us to several little bases in what had become the democratic republic of Vietnam. There were three Voodoos between us... twin-engined, single-seat McDonnell RF-101s. Since we always flew two-ship formations, there was always a spare airplane in case of mechanical problems and we could take turns flying by controlling our own scheduling.

"Since all of the sorties we flew were up north, regardless of which direction we took off while flying in innocent looking close formation, we would soon drop down and turn toward the IP (initial point) for our target area. Once there, we'd drop really low, tree-top to about two-hundred feet, spread out into *tactical* formation and push it up to just under supersonic while watching out for each other a half-mile apart as we both got pictures... then head home. Often, when there was a lot of suspected anti-aircraft activity, we had to cover targets alone as we flew separate sorties so as not to attract too much attention. Disciplined radio contact was critical in minimizing attention while not losing track of each other. We were unarmed and the only protection we had was surprise and speed at low altitude. We could easily go 'super' if it were not for the attention 'sonic-booms' created. We saved the afterburners for when we needed them because they ate up fuel too fast.

"There were several other SEATO nations helping in mutual support in those early days, but we learned to depend heavily on the Australians. They were a pleasure to work with and we were beginning to figure out what the Chinese were trying to accomplish when all of a sudden a lot of Americans started to show up and the 'Aussies' pulled out. Evidently the treaty had fallen apart. It seems American politicians and 'appointees' had their own ideas about how to do things... never mind what people in the theater of operations were saying, what was important to the politicians' careers was what the people in the newspapers were saying!

"We had learned a great deal during those first three months before everyone started getting organized on both sides of *the conflict* and they wanted us back Stateside to do some teaching and training without being obvious. The equipment coming south out of China was becoming more sophisticated as the USSR started expanding their supply. The more advanced systems were coming from Russian technology.

Pebbles of JADE

Something big was about to happen... based on the escalation we were observing.

"The next thing I knew I had a SAC, Strategic Air Command assignment at McConnell AFB learning to fly B-47s. At first I was upset. I was a fighter pilot... *not* a bomber pilot! However, I soon learned what they were doing and it wasn't so bad. The airplane *was* pretty. After they got me checked out and 'combat ready' as a co-pilot, they sent me to a special 'intelligence' school to help design tactics for low-altitude, high-speed, medium bomber sorties over what was now North Vietnam... and, no, it was *not* going to be nuclear. Some of the guys thought that one nuke in Haiphong Harbor might end everything quickly... including their *will to make war.* Others, more influential, thought it might easily start a nuclear WW-III.

"The B-47 was much sleeker and over a hundred knots faster than a B-52 at low altitude because it did not have such a large tail and was much more agile. The problem with high altitude bombing was that the missiles they were getting from the Soviets could reach up and shoot us down. They were getting more accurate and were starting to go higher. At least the B-52s could still stay above them. Also, from higher altitudes the terrain was deceptive. Southern Laos, for instance, looked remarkably like the *River of No Return Wilderness Area* in Idaho. However, unlike when Sacajawea was leading Lewis and Clark through the northern Rockies, just across the border Vietnam was bristling with SAM II missiles that could almost 'reach out and touch' in ways America's first family-tribal immigrants on our continent could not even dream of. The United States government does *not* have a history of taking over and settling in other countries, but the Communist countries sure don't seem to mind doing that. They seem to *live* by Darwin's *survival of the fittest* mentality... and then claim humans are *improving*! They call their push for dominance 'inevitable' and the 'best thing to do for the most people'. Sort of the same thing all socialist-thinking people have always said as they dream of creating some utopia. Even England is discovering it does not work, at least not in this lifetime because of greed and selfishness, but 'die-hards' die hard.

"My next assignment was to help develop special 'clip-in' packages to replace the nuclear weapons with 'iron' bombs and anti-personnel 'egg-carton' loads. I was a 'special weapons' instructor pilot who always was in the back-seat as co-pilot to train aircraft-commanders in the unique procedures we had developed. I had to be 'qualified' in the airplane, so I was able to get one of those special SAC 'spot promotions' to Captain about a year before I would have normally been eligible.

They had a name for me because I had such a unique job in our Bomb Wing... I floated between three different squadrons. Partly because of my previous experience coupled with what I was now more *mysteriously* doing... they called me 'Voodoo'.

"*That* is what I was doing on Guam... getting the guys ready to go. When everyone was ready, a B-52

Pebbles of JADE

wing would relieve them of their strategic mission with targets in China and they would start flying tactical missions to the southeast. China was setting the stage, with Soviet assistance, to 'absorb' Vietnam. From there they would be in position to expand west to Cambodia, Laos and when strong enough, Thailand and Taiwan (formerly Formosa). They had to be quickly and militarily stopped for the sake of all the people in those small, democratic nations. No one wanted more slavery, as the Soviets had done in the Eastern-bloc nations.

"About then, Typhoon Karen headed for Guam and we evacuated for Okinawa… and everything changed… *especially* my life."

Su-mei stood up and just looked at Peter while Paul continued.

"Peter, how much do they know? I'm on a *roll*. I think I have to stop here don't I?"

"Yeah, probably," said Peter. "But how you got into China no longer needs to be 'classified'… Polly, did you have something to ask?"

"No, Grandfather. Only I think the children are ready for their baths before going to bed. Their prayer-time is in forty-five minutes so they can be in bed by twenty-thirty."

"You have these kids using 'military time'? Paul smiled and asked.

"It is the international twenty-four hour clock the military uses," Su-mei responded. "You should know that, Paul. We are just trying to get our family ready for the rest of the world. They use 'AM' and 'PM'

American time when they are with their friends and at school. Here at *Jade West,* 'Brigadoon', you will find them using the metric system, speaking Chinese and practicing beautiful penmanship in kanji characters as well as in English… and much more.

"Polly, I'll work with the girls so the others can join Uhara-san in the *great room*."

The two older girls came out while Su-mei vanished into the kitchen. Soon the sound of a *herd* of little feet could be heard clamoring up the twenty-seven steps to their dormitory upstairs in the old converted railroad depot that was their home.

"Uhara-san," said Elizabeth as the other girls found places to sit. "Does anything you just told us have anything to do with the terrible nuclear events that happened in China and America a few years ago?"

"Nobody knows for sure," Paul began. "One thing certain is that in some way it was all somehow connected with the 'world domination' thinking of Communist ideology. Theories that don't take into account reality of the human heart, do not work and ultimately do not survive. In this case it did not take into account the human desire for 'freedom'.

"Have any of you read or been taught any of what I was talking about in your school books or classes?"

A pretty, tall, athletic looking girl who was just sitting down on the floor said, "A little, but we know it is not enough and many things have been left out. We're not sure why."

Another girl, fairly well endowed with sandy colored hair added, "I just don't think many of them,

Pebbles of JADE

the teachers, know much themselves. Instead of simply giving us information from history and letting us think about it, they keep trying to tell us *how* we should be thinking. Many history books have a lot of wrong information in them, and the teachers don't catch it. They seem to always want to be in control of how we think. I don't know… its weird."

Jade Bright jumped in with "Most of the high school teachers *are* weird! Oops, I'm sorry, Polly, I talk too much. Even my teachers in junior high tell me that… that I talk too much. They say *I* am weird."

"Sisters," said Elizabeth, "please introduce yourselves as you speak to Uhara-san. It will help him get to know us… and remember us."

"Voodoo Uhara-san."

"Yes, Anna Jade-san," answered Paul, smiling. He was so pleased he'd remembered her name.

"You never told us *why* and exactly *when* you were in China, where you lived or for how long. Also, how old is Pirate Pete?"

Peter put his head down and thought as he sipped his Sake. He turned to Elizabeth and asked if she could heat the Sake again a little for him and she immediately and silently saw to it… noticing he must be taking very small sips.

Skipping over a lot… he started, "I had a Chinese wife and lived there for many years in my young professional life getting an education in Chinese culture. It was an unofficial part of my work and I should not talk too much about it. I came back to American after my wife died, which was before everything changed over there. I guess that was my 'stealth-voodoo era'. As for old Pete, I think he's in his mid to late eighties.

The tall girl stood up and said, "Uhara-san, I am Meili Jade Rose, I am one year younger than Polly, but I have not been here as long as Ling Sao Jade Fragrant. My parents came from Kunming before I was born, but died while visiting in Taipei at the time of the *evil attack*. Ling Sao and I are both juniors in high school this year and have become interested in computer science. However, we have also been searching the Internet for family history. In the process we have found ancient Chinese, and considerably less-ancient Western writings, that have drawn us into desiring a more philosophical understanding of life on this earth. May we read something to you and learn your thoughts?"

"What does this have to do with anything I can tell you?" asked Paul, a little perplexed. "I never thought of myself as a philosopher, just someone trying to stay alive and do what was 'right' at the moment. You should talk to Grandfather Peter, he's more educated than I."

Su-mei responded, "They have, Paul. I think they want some 'second opinions' and they do not really trust their school-teachers because they seem to lack the wisdom of experience, or even much 'classical' education."

"I'll try," said Paul.

The sandy-haired girl stood. She was a beautiful, well-proportioned young woman who appeared to have

Pebbles of JADE

some mixed blood… even though her dark green blouse had a Chinese collar. In fact, she was a bit of a 'knockout' and Paul suspected the boys must be crazy about her. "My name is Ling Sao and I am fourteen. The most recent piece of writing sister Meili, another friend of ours at school, and I have been studying we printed out and I have it here with me, may I read it to you?"

"Sure, but I warn you, it may be way over my head."

"From what we have been told of you, Uhara-san, we do not think so," said Meili as she nodded to Ling Sao and sat down again.

Ling Sao began to read…

BenOHADI

4

SHADOWLANDS

"Let us not despise one another, lest we be neglectful of ourselves. For no man ever yet hated his own flesh, but nourishes and cherishes it. And therefore God has given to us but one habitation, this earth, has distributed all things equally, has lighted one sun for us all, has spread above us one roof, the sky, made one table, the earth, bear food for us. And another table has He given far better than this, yet that too is one, (those who share our mysteries understand my words) one manner of Birth He has bestowed on all, the spiritual, we all have one country, that in the heavens, of the same cup drink we all. He has not bestowed on the rich man a gift more abundant and more honorable, and on the poor one more mean and small, but He has called all alike. He has given carnal things with equal regard to all, and spiritual in like manner. Whence then proceeds the great inequality of conditions in life? From the avarice and pride of the wealthy. But let not, brethren, let not this any longer be; and when matters of universal interest and more pressing necessity bring us together, let us not be divided by things earthly and the insignificant: I mean, by wealth and poverty, by bodily relationship, by enmity and friendship; for all these things are a shadow, nay less substantial than a shadow, to those who possess the bond of charity from above. Let us then preserve this unbroken, and none of those evil spirits will be able to enter in, who cause division in so perfect a union; to which may we all attain by the grace and loving-kindness of our Lord Jesus Christ, by whom and with whom, to the Father and the Holy Ghost, be glory, now and ever, and world without end. Amen."

Ling Sao folded the paper she was reading from and continued, "A man in the early Christian Church, John Chrysostom, who lived from 344 to 407, wrote this in what was recorded as 'Homily XV' which I think means sermon number fifteen. Uhara-san, after listening to our Grandparents, as we know them, speak of you before you came, Meili and I thought your experience has made you more knowledgeable of the 'shadowland' he spoke of more than many people. And, after listening to you for the last couple hours, we knew we should talk to you about this a little. We have found most of the adults we talk to cannot seem to think deeply enough to begin any discussion. We also think the younger ones just wish to hear stories, so if you

Pebbles of JADE

prefer, this can be discussed later among a smaller group of those interested in applied transcendent psychology."

Paul definitely wanted to get into this kind of conversation, but was totally caught off-guard by this coming from one of these girls. He had not been around such *thinking* people since his days in China when such philosophical conversations were the norm with his friends every evening in someone's home. His mind started to drift back in his memories...

No one in the Shanghai district where he lived had a television until just before he left and outside entertainment was always a special occasion. When evening discussions with friends were not available, there was often some book smuggled in by a tourist to read. He had even once found a stash of old books from before Mao's revolution and soon discovered the lack of cosmopolitan education certainly did not diminish his friends' basic intelligence quotient. Even the few he'd suspected to be in the American *intelligence* community were always too busy solving problems to have such conversations... and here is this unique bunch of American high school girls! He was astonished... then realized he was sitting there with his Sake cup raised halfway to his mouth, frozen, just looking stupid.

"You are so right and it seems this John, whatever his name was from fifteen hundred years ago, understood with a great deal of insight. You have the advantage of having had some time to study what he said. Presumably, you picked that out from among many writings by others to concentrate on. I *am* impressed. Where did you get that material? Is that from a school textbook?"

Ling Sao, pointing to the east wall of floor-to-ceiling bookshelves: "No, not from our school... from our own small library of books that would be censored at school. We have a thirty-eight-volume set of such writings that have only been translated from the Greek within the last century... and they even include those thoughts identified by the rest of them, unanimously, as *heretical*. We have found them to be most interesting to browse through because they make all the different denominations in the United States, with all their different *spins* on Christianity, seem superfluous."

"I don't quite know how to respond and will have to think about what he said for a while. May I have that paper and read it this evening so I can collect my thoughts? I felt, as I listened, that he was 'hitting the nail on the head' and only wished I could have had his writings available many years ago when I was with people who enjoyed and learned from such discussions. Would you mind?"

"Not at all, Uhara-san," said Meili as she rose and got the paper from Ling Sao to give to him. Paul rose to meet her and realized she was taller than he was. Ling Sao saw him looking at her, chuckled and said, "Meili Jade intimidates many of the boys in school by her height, even though she is very light, not overweight. I think this is why they elected me and not her to the cheerleading squad... they wanted her on the

Pebbles of JADE

girls' basketball team. By the way, she is a very good player."

Anna jumped into the conversation with, "And she can really jump *high*!"

One of the other younger girls added, "That's because she's not white and not a boy."

Everyone laughed as Anna came back with, "But girls are not supposed to be able to whistle or jump and she can do both!"

The other girl shot back, "I can whistle, too!"

Polly stood up and everyone stopped talking. "Let's call it a 'wrap' for tonight, sisters. Tomorrow is Saturday, Grandmother says we can call it our first 'Distinguished Guest Holiday' and have Uhara-san all to ourselves all day." A little *cheer* went up, then Elizabeth continued with, "Wakeup time and chores will be normal but breakfast will not be until eight, to give Uhara-san a little time to be comfortable. It is now twenty-one hundred, later than normal for us, so get ready and come back down. Evening prayers will be at twenty-one thirty. **Go!**"

Everyone vanished and Peter led Paul to the north end of the building downstairs where there was a large room with two beds, one single and one double. Also there was a small couch, coffee table, rocking chair, floor-lamp... and a fireplace already lit for him. Evidently this was the guest bedroom. There was also a private door that opened out to the river-view deck in back.

As he closed the door to the room that would be his for the next couple weeks, the paper Meili had given

BenOHADI

him still in his hand, he knew this was going to be a most interesting visit and that he certainly had much to think about. Feeling very tired, he sat on the couch and pulled off his shoes. These people really had something! It seemed to be an enriched life of some kind that he could not remember ever seeing in a family… in America or China. If they represented the *new generation*, maybe there was some hope. They all seemed ambitious! He unpacked, used the downstairs restroom in the hallway outside his room, dressed for bed, propped a pillow up on the double bed and started reading the girls' paper, musing with excitement about what tomorrow's conversations held.

JAIRUS' DAUGHTERS

He knew he had slept well when he woke up dreaming of floating through the air. The same feeling he used to have long ago when easily flying over mountain ridges just above the ground in a 'recce' Voodoo... the feeling of the airplane actually being a mechanical extension of his own body. There used to be this local Saigon radio station that played classical music he could usually pick up on his ADF (AM, broadcast band, directional finding) radio. He would keep the volume low so he could hear communications on tactical frequencies. The lilting strains of a Strauss waltz or a Bach Brandenburg Concerto would give him a rhythm to 'jink' to for a short period of time when anticipating ground fire... assuming the gunners were not also listening to the same, rhythmical music. It had always, pleasantly worked for him... and what he awoke to was "Jesu, joy of man's desiring" being played on the piano at the other end of the big building. Soon it stopped and he decided it was time to get up. He had not closed any curtains and could see the sun lighting some remaining snow up on the peaks of what he had been told was 'West Mountain' from his window overlooking the deck. His fireplace had died during the night and he could feel the room air was quite cool. It was summer! Did it always get this cool at night up here? That must be why they'd lit the fire for him last night... and why there was a small pile of wood, kindling, newspaper and matches stacked next to it. He knew he wanted a shower, but decided he should light a fire again first so the room would be warm when he returned to dress. Then he remembered being told he would have to wait till all the girls were downstairs so he could go up and use one upstairs in their dormitory, because there was something wrong with the one downstairs. He could wait.

As he finished dressing and was leaving his room, the piano music began again... a "minuet"? Bach... maybe even Chopin? His knowledge of classical music was not that great, but he remembered how popular Bach music was in China and it brought back fond memories. It was so 'rich' and had such a calming effect on his psyche. All the mathematicians he had known worked so efficiently while listening to it... and then there were the private 'concerts' coming from windows in the evenings as he walked down the humble, narrow streets in those days. A few homes did have some little pianos. He could just imagine Su-mei or Elizabeth sitting at the 'grand' he'd seen in the *great room* the night before. As he came from the hallway into the room he saw their *refectory* table being set for breakfast, but he could see no one at the piano... yet he could hear it. He was sure it was not a recording... maybe they had one of those CD gadgets hooked up to the piano. Then there was a *wrong* note and it stopped. As he walked around it he finally saw the little girl hidden by the music book. She seemed startled, looked down and put her hands between her legs. He had seen her last night, but she was one of only a few in group-two who had not said a word. "I am sorry. I made a

Pebbles of JADE

mistake. And I hope my practicing did not wake you up."

"You play beautifully. Thank you. I enjoy listening to you. How old are you?"

She jumped off the bench, faced him while standing very erect and said, "I am thirteen, my name is Mei-ch'en Jade Beauty. My family raised me in the misty valleys of Kweilin, but brought me to Malaysia after I was ten. Robbers killed them one night, but I was rescued by a Singapore family who sent me here after finding out my relatives in Taipei died. Jade East had not yet been started in Taiwan. Please forgive me for saying so much… and for not introducing myself last night."

Paul just nodded and asked her what she had been playing while puzzling over how young she looked and old she sounded.

"I am trying to learn Bach's minuet in D minor. I am afraid I have much more practicing to do."

"I was impressed. How long have you been playing… and how can you make your fingers reach the chords?"

"My father played in our symphony orchestra and my mother taught piano. I have been practicing for as long as I can remember and I now I wish to do as my mother did, have a family and teach music… And, my fingers do *not* reach, which makes me have to use a trick my teacher taught me and messes up my timing."

"Do you have any sisters or brothers?"

"Yes, I had one much older brother, but he died in China. My parents were trying for another boy and I have one older sister who is now an orphan like me in Guling at Jade Far East. I would like to return to the province I was born in and see her again someday. My parents had left her to help our grandmother when they tried to get out with me. They told me they would get her out after grandmother was gone... but they died first. Now grandmother is dead and the Benjamins are my grandparents. It's okay. They will help me.

Paul watched Elizabeth open the front door and clang an old cowbell outside. "What is that?" he asked.

"Oh, Polly is telling everyone to come in from chores, that breakfast is ready. Are you not familiar with this old American custom?"

"I remember reading about ranches in the old west doing that for their hired help, that must be where it came from. Most folks didn't do that in the cities I lived in."

Soon about half a dozen girls were crowding around an outside faucet to dust off their jeans and rinse their hands... and then coming in to the downstairs washroom to clean up a little better. Peter and Su-mei came in behind them doing the same thing. "What have they been doing?" Paul asked.

"Some are doing yard work, others have gardening projects and I think they might be getting a deck-repair project ready to go this afternoon. There is also one horse on loan to water, feed and take care of."

"Why are you not helping?"

"I will later. We also take turns practicing our music lessons so we are not all trying to do the same thing at the same time."

Pebbles of JADE

"Oh. Do many of you play the piano?"

"Quite a few. Some of us also play the violin and other instruments. We all take lessons of some kind... just as all of us are in different language classes. We also have classes in homemaking skills. On Sunday evenings we have fun with what used to be called 'finishing school' in the Western countries. Jade East and Far East also have the same kind of classes, but their 'finishing school' part of it is geared to the Chinese culture."

As they moved to the big table Paul was dazzled by this tiny person he was talking to as an adult... but had more questions. "Do you ever have any of your friends from school out here? I'll bet this is quite different from what they're used to."

"Oh yes. But not this weekend, because of you. Whenever we have others join us they just have to fit into our schedule. They do not *have* to do the chores if there is something else they would rather do, but most of them want to because it is an easy way to learn to do different things they never get to do at home.

"If any of our sisters are staying overnight at anyone's house on Friday nights, which is the only night we are allowed to do so, then we get to take turns inviting our friends to stay with us... and use their vacant bed. Most of our friends have been able to do that because their parents consider Brigadoon to be so safe. Sometimes we invite the whole Church congregation out for a picnic after our worship service on Sunday. Lots of people come because, for some reason, they really like it out here and our grandparents like for us to mingle with the older people. Everyone likes the fresh vegetables from our garden... but, we only do that in the summer when we can be outdoors."

Su-mei spoke up, "Let's pray and then you know the rules. Please excuse me girls, but for Uhara-san's sake I must explain... After everyone has eaten whatever they want, we can sit and talk as long as we want. Those on kitchen duty will keep hot tea and coffee on the table, but we are all responsible for putting our dirty dishes in the sink for rinsing so the kitchen staff can clean them in the dishwasher. It is Saturday. We like to think of the *Sabbaoth*, so everyone is free for the rest of the morning and afternoon. Exercise is at the normal time... but optional. A light, 'help-yourself' lunch will be laid out at noon and everyone who has not been excused is to be back in the house to clean up for dinner by seventeen hundred. Those assigned to kitchen duty must be here by sixteen hundred."

As everyone found a chair around the table and took each others' hands, Mei-ch'en quickly explained to Paul, "We each get 'duty' for a meal about twice a week. It's fair... and we don't have to do other chores on those days, but most of us do anyway, because we have fun when we're together... it's not like work."

"You say they do the same things at Jade East and Jade Far East?"

"Yes, that's what we're told. I'm sure there are some variations."

"Have any of you been to any of the other *Jade* homes?"

Pebbles of JADE

"No, but we all want to… and they want to come here. We keep in touch by E-mail regularly and all feel we know… and want to meet each other."

After a short, but very sincere prayer of thanksgiving, everyone sat down. Unlike what Paul expected in a *boarding house* it was quite orderly as the food was passed around and called for. The kitchen staff did not eat and evidently they ate while preparing and afterwards. Even the conversations were not particularly loud. He remembered his military days… this was quite different. But then, these were girls and they were deliberately being taught manners. Not bad.

While he was eating he watched them all. They were going to be world-travelers, no doubt. But he, too, wanted to learn about the other *Jade* homes. He had only heard about this one from 'old Pete' because this was where Peter and Su-mei were. Now he was learning there were more. He must talk to Peter more. They never really had a chance to catch up on their old Air Force days at Mountain Home before the world as they knew it was rattled to its core. He did not think anything could surpass the experience he had in China forty years earlier, but the *Almost War*, as most people referring to that event were now calling it, certainly did. These kids could make a difference, especially since they were from both the countries that were directly involved.

The food was good and he said so. Su-mei proudly introduced the two cooks who had prepared everything all by themselves. One was the fourteen year-old 'cheerleader', Ling Sao, and her assistant was six year-old Lili. They smiled and went back to work. Amazing. He looked at Peter and said, "Who wouldn't want to marry one of these girls!"

Peter responded with a smile, "Why do you think I feel so blessed... and embarrassed? I can't do what these girls can do, and the young guys will have to wait a little. Don't rush them. These girls all want to take their turns visiting the others first... their overseas sisters. Jade East in Taiwan may have to wait. They are just getting started and settling in... and they are still suffering a great pain of loss, plus there is still some radioactive cleanup to do. Jade Far East is a different story. They are well established in the Mount Lushan region city of Guling and the girls there are all from the mainland of China. They call themselves 'Jairus' Daughters', because in light of the horrendous number of deaths all around them they each feel they have been saved from death for a while... similar to the Biblical story. They are very ambitious, just like the Polly Brigade. By the way, they also refer to Jade Far East, *Shangri-La,* as 'Cana' from the children of Abraham history. Su-mei and I just came back from spending a year over there getting that one set up."

"A year? Who ran this place?"

"Elizabeth and the 'Polly Brigade'."

"Were they safe?"

"The Christian congregation and the whole town kept the guys away from here... they actually kept a rotating guard duty going around this place, staying in our house over there, plus... Well, why don't we take our coffee outside and watch their morning workout.

Come on. You've got to see this. The local guys don't mess with these girls and, in fact, are so long-term interested in them that they protect them from outsiders… while at the same time they are seriously developing some career-goals for themselves to impress them. Come on, they have just changed clothes and are getting started. Some of the other girls in their school classes are starting to regularly join them. That strikingly good-looking girl next to Su-mei is Elona, one of those local girls who is smart and liked by *Brigadoon* a lot. She may show up in some of the sessions you have with the older girls because she is so smart… she wants to be a doctor."

There they all were, gathering on the lawn… dressed in *sweats*. Out front was Su-mei beginning the stretching exercises. After about five minutes they were all quickly getting synchronized. Then Su-mei started shouting instructions and some very intense Jujitsu began. This brought back memories of his youth in Hawaii and his years in China.

Peter reminded him that Su-mei, before he met her while she was working for the FBI in San Francisco, had been a teacher for young girls and mothers in Chinatown. Being a judo instructor was the cover for what she and her family were doing at *Chaing's Wok,* the family restaurant, and the old *Opium Den* nightclub next door. Paul remembered. That was when he was being held by "Immigration" officials after buying his way out of China and it embarrassed him to remember that during that time, he thought Su-mei was a *stripper!* "Elizabeth is just about good enough to take over, and

Su-mei wants to get back to Guling for a short visit to see how they are doing with all their various instruction over there, while she can leave her protégé in charge here. They can stay in touch via Internet. We will lose her when she graduates from school in Cascade and goes to visit the other *Jade* homes. Meili and Ling Sao are coming right along and will also be ready to take over in a couple years. We would like Elizabeth to take over some duties with *Jairus' Daughters*. We would also like to bring some of the older girls over here for a while so we can acquaint them better with the English language, American customs and true history. We hope to get all these girls at all three *Jade houses* interactive in real life, as well as on web-sites, because there is a lot they can do. They also are all anxious to do so, which is exciting to us, considering what they, and all in our two countries have been through!"

5

SEER SCHOOL

The Karate training exercises and drills lasted about two hours, with some girls leaving and others joining at various times, apparently to accommodate their other schedules. There was always someone playing the piano, violin, flute or oboe in the background. Even though school had started again, there were occasional rubber rafts and canoes passing by on the river whose occupants would always catch sight of the activities of this large group of girls on the grassy, lower-lawn. Always… there was a lot of excited pointing, shouting and waving, sometimes some furious paddling against the current as they watched this unexpected and unusual sight. The days were still sunny and they were soon down to their shorts and tank-tops after getting warmed up… and all appeared well tanned. These girls were in remarkably good condition, from the eldest down to the littlest… and they were having a great deal of fun! Paul certainly was impressed… it made him feel very young *and* very old at the same time. Had they not been interested in him, it could have been depressing to keep remembering again how old he really was.

"Peter, do they do this every morning?"

"Only in the summer. As the weather starts to cool, it is really cold in the mornings and they do their exercises inside. On Saturdays they have their Karate a little later at ten hundred, then clean up for lunch. In mid-winter they go outside on nice days... but stay in their 'sweats', naturally."

Hesitantly, Paul asked, "Do any of the older ones have boyfriends?"

"Oh yeah! However, their schedules are severely restricted. That would cause rebellion for most girls, I suppose, but not with these girls because of the 'peer-pressure' of their sisters. Also, there is cultural pride as they can see the Western nations' social breakdown while their own cultural heritage is rebounding in such a healthy way. Their schoolteachers are divided. We think many actually hate them, while others adore them. Let's not get into politics. Suffice it to say the end of a monopolistic union helped, but that change began less than a generation ago."

"What will happen when they leave here?"

"Some want so go on with a university or technical education, but not all. The State government's school system painfully lacks very much in any home-economics teaching, social or cultural refinement... so we try to make up for that lack and add an historical Christian education with our own additional home schooling... and uncensored little library. We don't practice the 'politically correct' censorship the government education system has learned to endure. They all *will* do one thing first upon graduation. It has already been budgeted. Each will visit *Jade East* in

Taiwan, then spend a year at *Jade Far East* on the mainland, which they regularly refer to as the *Middle Kingdom*. One or two may elect to stay and work at one of the *Jade Houses*, the others will get married or go to more school or both. They are free to do whatever they want and we will help as their *family* in any way they would like us to. We do not want to establish the *Jade Houses* as some sort of economic institution. Too much of that has already been done by the U.S.'s Christian denominations."

"What about the ones finishing school in China? What will they do?"

"They, too, will visit the other *Jade homes*, then proceed with their own plans. These kids all want to travel and see things. In a way, that is intimidating to many of the other school children they associate with who have often not even been out of southern Idaho. They know they are different and constantly battle with their unwanted pride. Many of their friends in school, and even some teachers, constantly ask them if they don't get tired of always being told what to do. They explain patiently how fortunate they are, but it can be tough. Tenacity is a virtue."

Peter continued, laughing to himself at how he was, sort of, getting back at Paul, "Those in the Chinese *Jade* 'homes' want to see America, especially the old West and Midwest… they don't seem too interested in seeing the high-density population areas. Those in the U.S. want to see their 'homeland'. More of them than we expected want to attend the 'Seer School' that started last year in Guling near *Jade East*."

"Some of the girls have mentioned that... what is it?"

"Well, I cannot remember the Chinese name for it, but it is actually two different dormitory-style homes on the east side of the mountain city between East Valley and the Botanical Garden area on the way to Ponyong Lake. Today they are Orthodox Christian study centers originally established by some Eastern Church monks, but they are not seminaries leading to any clergy-status. However, they must not marry, or even date, while attending. For two years a student must live a celibate life. They are divided for men and women. Sort of a 'monastery' and a 'convent' kind of life."

"Why would any of these girls want to enter a 'convent'?"

"That surprised us. Patience seems to be in their blood. They started hearing from different boys and girls that have already started attending, through connections made with other girls at *Jade Far East*. Two girls have even become engaged to be married when they finish. The boys are attending the men's school and the girls are at the women's. From what I gather, it is sort of a worship and prayer oriented Bible school that studies the historical, traditional understandings of the Apostolic Succession of the Faith... not so much the American Evangelical spin on the Church. The only *Head of the Church* is King Jesus. There is a great deal of emphasis on the Trinity, especially the Holy Spirit, but they insist they are *not* Pentecostal, only serious about early-Church teachings regarding the mysterious enhanced *Life* associated with their reconnection to the God of the Universe. They call it 're-*ligament*-ing.' They also seem to have a very zealous 'mission' spirit. What seems to be attracting them and other Christians to it in the first place is the beauty of their worship... not songs, but harmonized 'liturgical' singing... a cappella. They only use a piano, violin, cello, guitar, flute or almost any other solo instrument when they are singing hymns. Those reporting from Guling say the timeless, beautiful liturgy, that ties all the changing parts of their worship services together, just makes one 'melt' inside. They say it not only ties them together, but also to others around the world and throughout time. Su-mei and I look forward to visiting and hearing this. Evidently, it is something they claim they have been polishing for two thousand years and many all over the world, in certain Christian denominational circles, are familiar with it in a 'shadowy' sort of way. They know they are all connected in the faith in the Messiah, Christ the eternal Tao. They are working hard to implement that practice at the parish in town."

Paul was looking puzzled. "Now you've raised a lot of questions in my mind. But you still haven't answered. Why do they want to do this? What are their goals? Are you sure you two are not pressuring them in some way?"

"No, really, no one seems to be pressuring them... and it does not seem to be for all of them. The *goal* seems to be to strive to do all they *can*, all that is available to them, for the sake of 'changing the world'. They're very ambitious and do not want to see what

BenOHADI

happened... happen again. Talking among themselves upstairs at night, they have concluded that terrorism in the world came about through the whispers of evil to the hearts of Zarathustra, Mohamed, Hitler, Marx and Lenin, Mao and Stalin, Bin Ladin and all that have anti-Christ submissive weaknesses... and what almost happened a couple years ago, could happen again. The girls know wars are caused by someone wanting to be in 'control'... followed by retaliation, retribution and revenge. The 'endless cycles' must be stopped. They know 'power' and 'greed' and 'lust' are somehow related in the secular world... that 'might' is associated with the military or money.

"These girls just seem to be very compassionate and do not trust what the Devil has done to people's minds in, what *they* call, 'AC societies' (meaning, anti-Christian). Believe me Paul, I'm not making this up! The girls sit down and tell us all this and we're outnumbered. We just sit and listen. Elizabeth once told me she wants to educate the world regarding what works and does not work. She's tired of all the stupidity and wants every bit of the deep-magic of God that He says she can use, she does not want to *ignore* people or the problem. Sometimes Su-mei and I just look at each other and try to figure out what's going on."

"They really talk about all that stuff? How do you keep up with them? That's pretty heavy stuff. But then I guess all those nukes the Peoples Liberation Army of the old regime set off in their misguided attempt to take over the U.S. in conjunction with North Korea was pretty heavy stuff too, considering all the lives lost. Good thing politically correct communism has all but disappeared, maybe the world can get back to what 'works' again."

"That's what she says she and the others want to do, help the Chinese get back to the original *middle*, not just half-way back. They know that *not* all of their history was good. They want to learn from history what would work best in modifying their culture... without totally losing what was originally good about their cultural ancestry. They know moving away from Shang-ti did not work well at all, so they want to help their people move closer to their original God... the One reflected in their original written language. We think their ambitions are noble and an example of practical thinking, so we cheer them on, while encouraging them to not scare others off with religious zealotry. They have no idea of the anti-God religious opposition they will run into... especially from the nations of other tongues in the world that see U.S. and China now being vulnerable to their own evil, expansionist greed. What these girls seem to be learning in their studies is the U.S. and the *new* Middle Kingdom of o*ld* China are now actually stronger than before because their people themselves are pulling together again with hearts free from intimidation. Also, now that so many anti-God people are gone, those left are not so predisposed to rejecting the power God offers people *reconnected* in a 'new birth' of a new *Israel* of the *Faith* of Abraham, Jacob and Mary. This is different than just the *Jacobites* of his human bloodline, even if it could be proven."

Realizing he was on a *roll,* as his friend had been earlier, Peter sat on one of the benches surrounding the trees growing through the deck. "Paul, I'm sorry if I sound more 'religious' than you expected, but I'm getting old… and maybe I don't care so much any more how people think of me. Let me tell a *recent* story. One of our girls was almost raped by several drunken visitors from out of town one evening after a ballgame. At the last minute they all ran off! Then were caught by the local football team who *just happened* to be leaving the gym. She was shouting and soon told them what had happened. Her clothes were badly torn from her fight with them and upon being captured the young men ultimately confessed. When asked why they suddenly ran off they said it was because of 'three enormous, powerful looking men that ran up to help her.' *She* never saw anyone else! No one has ever been able to corroborate who it was these guys might have been. Our guys didn't know what to think. The Polly Brigade all thinks they were *angels*. I don't know what to think… our girls don't make up stuff. There are no reasons to doubt any of the details of the story given by anyone. That was when they started *seriously* talking about the 'Seer School' as something that might be important for them if they want to be of help in changing the world's reaction to Shang-ti's merciful grace. What more could God do if allowed by more people in more hearts? You think our girls are becoming some kind of religious nuts?"

Pebbles of JADE

Paul just sat there, poured more tea for Peter and himself and listened to the girls vigorously shouting during their exercises. "Could she not have just fought them off? Look at them, they're good."

"She tried. They were pretty badly bruised, but were big and one of them hit her from behind with a brick. She said the next thing she knew some guy was on her tearing at her clothes while the others held her down. All of a sudden they all started shouting and ran. She didn't know why. There was no one around. She just lay there for a few seconds trying to calm down, then scrambled to get her dropped bags together when she saw someone come out the side door of the gym. She shouted to them, they recognized her, understood what she hollered, jumped in their cars and actually caught the guys. She later identified them in a police lineup. That's when the rest of the story came out and the girls started getting serious about this Seer School *idea*."

Su-mei clapped her hands and the girls all stopped what they were doing and listened to her. Soon they were all headed for the showers. "Oh no," said Peter. "I blew it. I should not have kept you here... you could have been using a shower. Now there won't be any hot water left. We have a couple big hot water heaters, but it will take an hour after they are all finished. I'm sorry, Paul. Can you wait till after lunch?"

"If all of you can stand me, of course. I would not have missed any of this for all the tea in China," he laughed. "Do many people know anything about everything you've been telling me?"

"No. People still generally resist talk about God. They think it is just 'religion' and in a way it is... in the true etymological sense of 're-ligation' or 'ligature' of a ligament that was torn apart. When there are no 'quacks' involved it is very practical exercise for humans. The Russians have even put the Orthodox priests back to work because it will help in the long run to morally 'heal' their society. I don't think the officials really believe in God."

Su-mei came up the stairs from the lawn by the river. She was wiping herself down with a towel, but she did not look as if she had even been sweating and did not sound tired at all as she spoke briefly with Peter. Paul disliked himself for noticing it, but could not get over what a gorgeous body she had! His old flying buddy was truly a fortunate man at his age. Paul knew him to be a little younger than himself, but he must be at least seventy and *she* didn't even look thirty... although he knew *she* must be pushing forty by now. Turning to him Su-mei asked, "Would you like to work out with us Monday? There are never men in our group and we would love to have you join us. It will just be very early calisthenics exercise so they can make the school bus on time. Karate will begin again next Saturday."

"Su-mei, it has been many years since I kept up the regimen. But, what the heck, yes. I need to get back in shape a little." (He patted his less-than-flat stomach.) "Please let me be excused after five or ten minutes as I first try to get back into a *little* better shape... I would not want to die out there on you! I used to regularly work out in some similar routines and it would be fun to get back into it. I take it you do not work out on Sundays?"

"No. We rest on Sundays. No chores or even homework during the school-year, but you will get to hear the *Tamarac Sisters* work out a little."

"Hear? Who are they?"

"Three to five of our girls harmonize as liturgy-leaders during Sunday worship… did Peter tell you where they got the idea to start doing that?"

"No… Yes! He mentioned something about some girls learning to harmonize."

"Good. Well they're them. On Sunday afternoon they get together with one on the piano or guitar and they sing old Andrews Sisters and McGuire Sisters songs just for fun while teaching some of the younger ones how to harmonize. It's a lot of fun. One of them is even learning to play a bugle quite well for 'The Boogie Woogie Bugle Boy of Company B'. The town likes to use them for opening various events the community puts on. They are really very popular. They even open all the town and school ballgames by singing, in harmony, the National Anthem. I know you will enjoy it. I do. I am such a lucky woman to have all these talented girls and all of this!

"Let me run up and rinse off before lunch, if there's any hot water left," she waved as she headed into the stairway door.

"You are one lucky man, Peter."

"I know," he smiled and closed his eyes. "I thank God for all the 'luck' he gives me every day."

Paul looked down, moved his feet around a little and said, "In times past I would have been turned off by all this 'God-talk', but it just really seems different now, out here, with you folks and with everything that's been happening. I guess I'm changing... must be getting old... I'm not fighting it. I wonder how Yulin will take all this? I'll have to talk to her about it. All she was ever around in her childhood were what Americans in the western part of the U.S. might call 'Jack-Buddhists'. Old Pete doesn't seem to let conversations go that way, but I think he probably had a Christian upbringing of some kind, from some of the things he's said... just doesn't want to talk about it."

Peter looked up at the blue sky and puffy clouds. "Some people only think they are 'open-minded', but can't see the vision... or handle it very well. I think you'll be okay with your Yulin. All these girls will be praying for you... she doesn't stand a chance," he chuckled.

Want a cold beer with your lunch?"

"Sure!" Paul looked up with a smile. "Nobody minds?"

"No, not here. Bud-Light or Guinness Stout?"

"That's quite a spread. I'll have a Guinness... if it's not too cold."

"It will be cool... can't keep it warm in Idaho air."

"Cool! You must not have Lucas refrigerators out west."

DREAMERS

While they were finishing lunch on the deck, two cars drove up with a couple young mothers and their children... including the very calm, but self confident older girl they called Elona Li. She helped the older women *ride herd* on the little ones, while carrying bundles of supplies for them. Su-mei explained this was fairly typical on Saturdays because the children, schoolmates, enjoyed playing together out here. She excused herself and joined them, leaving Peter and Paul with their beers watching the various forms of water transportation headed down the river. A little discussion about flotation recreation, the advantages versus disadvantages of tubes, rafts, canoes and kayaks, with a little philosophical discourse on differing human personalities... then Paul noticed only one or two of the older girls were still around and asked where everyone was.

"They run around a little on Saturday. The younger ones are either riding their bikes up and down our road to the homes of some neighbors with kids along the bench overlooking the river just to the north, or they're playing in the farmer's field to the south. They know better than to get too near any cattle. The older ones usually go hiking in different directions, usually two-by-two... although some of them have to ride their bikes quite a ways before they get started."

"Where do they go?" asked Paul.

"Well, some of them like to hike up West Mountain to the lakes up there, but they ride their bikes to the base of the trails which are about three miles from here around the bottom end of the lake."

"The girls really stay in good physical shape, don't they? I noticed you don't have a TV out here, so I guess there are no 'couch-potatoes' in your unique crop of Idaho spuds…"

Taking in a deep breath of the clean mountain air, "By the way, what do they do with their bikes when they start climbing the mountain? And, are they rock-climbing or are there trails?"

Peter smiled. "The girls are pretty smart. What we call 'recreationists' to distinguish them from the real tourists, have stolen a couple bikes. They don't fly in, come up on busses or the train, but drive in from the Boise area. The girls have learned to hide the bikes in some pretty obscure places off the trails a little so they can't be seen from the new subdivisions, roads or trails. This past summer there were no problems. The real out-of-state tourists cause no particular problems. They usually have rental cars, not pickups, motor homes, trailers, campers or motorbikes hooked onto them. They are also much more appreciated by those trying to make a living up here because they come ready to spend, rather than bringing all their supplies with them from stores down below.

"As for the climbing, it's not steep. They use trails, but it is a fairly high altitude and gives them a lot of breathing and stamina exercise. Two or three always stay together… and they keep a cell-phone with them.

Pebbles of JADE

Ling Sao Jade is the only one I have concerns for because so many boys are attracted to her. She's the cheerleader."

"I noticed. What's her background, Peter? She's not pure Chinese, is she?"

"No," he answered. "Her mother was a 'Party' official who died with all the others. And all she ever told Ling was that her father was a Russian nuclear scientist and said he would come back some day... sort of a *Madam Butterfly* story. He never came back. Ling was twelve when we got her and she already spoke pretty good English. She's smart as a whip, so watch out. Curiously, we have *not* detected any pent-up anger in her. Yet, she seems to have her own agenda we can't figure out. We don't think *she* even knows what is 'driving' her. Her teachers like her, but seem a little intimidated. She quotes Tolstoy, Dostoevsky and Solzhenitsyn... sometimes in Russian. She's the only one we have who was truly raised as an atheist, until she discovered those Russian writers and the historical solidity of *their* faith."

"The others?"

"Buddhist."

"No Christians?"

"No, the Christians were not Communists with an 'in the closet' private faith. They were strong in their faith and did not abandon girls as the non-Christians so easily did... which is why we have them."

"Interesting," said Paul while staring at the river. "Long ago, in China, my wife said the Japanese were born Buddhist, lived their lives as Shinto because of all the ceremonies, then died as Buddhists again because of their belief in an 'afterlife'. Is there a Buddhist Temple around here?"

"No."

"Where do they go?"

"What do you mean?"

"Well, how do they keep up with their religion?"

Peter laughed, then said, "Their religion is Christianity. They've discovered the God of the Universe that Buddha was searching for when he said: 'I seek Truth.' They worship with us. They believe the words of Jesus, *'I AM the Truth...'* when he instructed his disciples."

"Is that fair? Are you 'converting' them?"

"Ask them. We have always told them that as long as we provide for them and they live with us, they are to attend worship services with us. If they do not believe what they hear, that's up to them. They are free to read and listen to whatever they want. Most of them already had been taught quite a bit about all of China's many ancient religious beliefs. If they only heard what the government schools teach, they would not have anything to choose between and would be steered into believing there was no God... or in America that every religion could be *true*... except the teachings of Jesus of Nazareth. No one can force anything on their hearts. They know they are free to *believe* as they please... and when they leave our home they are free to *do* as they please. We're training them to keep a *truly* open mind and to at least know what historic Christians believe to be true."

Pebbles of JADE

"Whose idea was it for the 'Tamarac Sisters' to sing in Church?"

"It was their own idea. Actually, it was Ling Sao who organized them. She got the idea from the Russian Orthodox Church and the U.S.O."

"The U.S.O.?"

"Yeah, she loved old movies with Abbot and Costello and Bob Hope."

"You're kidding… what's that got to do with Church?"

Chuckling. "No kidding… ask her."

"I will. She really has me curious. When can I talk to her… in fact, when can I talk to any of them? I thought they wanted to talk. Were they just patronizing me? Where are they?"

"They're out doing only a little of their usual Saturday stuff. They'll be back soon, I know… they *do* want to talk to you… we haven't told them much. You know you have plenty of time and there are only twelve of them… well, maybe thirteen. Elona Li is out biking with Ling Sao this morning and I know she wants to be in on everything going on out here also.

"Who *is* she?"

"She was adopted and raised by an older man and woman who say they are of a *Hebrew* clan called, I think she once said something like, "Mallek"… whoever they are. We only know what they've told us, which is not much. Their first names are Johann and Magdelena, they were both doctors doing medical research in Eisenach, Germany right after WW-II for forty years where they raised two sons. If I recall, their names were Martin and Sebastian. Coming to America with their adopted daughter, they first moved to Salem, Missouri… not far from St. Louis, and were General Family Practitioners for seven years before retiring at Lake Cascade three years ago. They moved to a very private little place up on Crown Point with a view of the Tamarack ski slopes… about the time Su-mei and I started this place up. Ling Sao thinks we should let Elona Li add *'Jade'* to her name also. Of course that's okay with us, if she wants to do that someday."

"Are they a Jewish family… with a Chinese daughter?"

Smiling. "No. They all worship with us… in fact, they are *very* active in the parish. He's the choir director, she plays the cello and sings with a beautiful soprano voice and occasionally he will do some solo or liturgical singing with his startling baritone voice. Their talent is amazing and enormously inspiring to other budding musical artists. On top of that, they contribute tirelessly to our local mission society, 'HIS'… which stands for *Hospitality In Service*. Many have volunteered their help in *hospice care*, *meals-on-wheels*, taxi-cab assistance, and there are even some licensed physical therapists… all free for those too old to work, invalids, or those otherwise infirmed."

"Wow! What about Elona?"

"She spends most of her time with the girls, and even with Su-mei during the workouts… and she's always been encouraging with me. Just as her parents are… she is also musically and artistically talented, and seems tireless. The girls respect her not only for her

Pebbles of JADE

valuable attention, but she always seems to be there when someone needs help. She even helped me once get out of a melancholy mood one time when I was thinking back to my early days with Leilani, the love of my life for many years before she died. This young Elona Li was *startling* in how she brought me back to remembering that God rescued her from pain and suffering, then provided me with Su-mei who is so much like she was with so many of the same strengths, it is uncanny. It's like Lei lives on through her. God is good. She helped bring back memories from two lifetimes that seemed to have merged into one. She's priceless!

"I suggest you let *all* these young people take you for 'walks'… one at a time. Get to know each of them personally. We've taught them it helps develop wise discipline and trust."

"That's a good idea. Would anyone mind… or get any wrong ideas?"

"I don't think so. They all know we trust you and would feel privileged. Do it!"

"Should I start with the kitchen staff that is still here?"

"No, they've not had a chance to get out yet today. Start with the first one who gets back from a walk, or a hike and climb, or from playing in the field. Even the little ones want to talk as soon as their friends and mothers leave. Don't rush them."

Just as he was saying that, onto the deck burst Lili shouting, "Where is Voodoo Uhara-san? I want to hear about China!"

Paul stood up, laughing, and grabbed her hand saying, "Take me for a walk and I'll tell you everything you want to know. You are Lili Jade Green, right? Where've you been… you're all sweaty?"

Lili had a smile that stretched from ear to ear with the whitest teeth Paul had ever seen. She looked at Peter and simply asked, "Grandpa?"

"Of course… Go, you two. Get out of here. Don't worry, I'll help clean up here. Lili, tell Uhara-san the dream you told Grandmother last night. I think he will like it."

Lili giggled with both hands over her mouth, then took Paul's hand and said, "Bye." Turning to Paul she led him off the north end of the deck somewhat aggressively. "Let's take off our shoes and walk up the river-bank where it's cool. We can turn back at the bridge. I've been racing. Wait till you hear my dreams!"

"You have had more then one?"

"Oh, yes. I have lots. They have really been fun. Sometimes I don't want to wake up, but I know I have to. If I try to go back to sleep later, it doesn't work… I don't get the dreams again. Some of the others get them in the mornings, too."

"Tell me about yours."

"They're about China."

"How old are you?"

"In my dreams, or now?"

"Now."

"Six, American style. Seven in China."

"How old were you when you came here?

Pebbles of JADE

"Four."

"Do you remember when you first arrived?"

"No, only that I started having dreams."

"You didn't have them before?"

"No."

"Do they bother you?"

"No, only... I want to understand them better."

"Tell me about them. Is there anything the same about them all?"

"There are always three boys in them. I think they might be my brothers. They're okay... we run and play a lot."

"Do you have brothers?"

"I don't know. *I* think so, but no one knows."

"If you have brothers, do you want to see them?"

"Maybe. I don't know," she said as she kind of screwed up her nose and mouth and spun around in circles as she walked, slinging her long black hair around like an umbrella. "It would be interesting, but it might mess up our lives. I don't really need to... just curiosity. I would like to *explain* my dreams to Grandma and Grandpa, but I don't know how."

"Why don't you call them 'Grandmother' and 'Grandfather' like the others?"

"I do, usually, to their face. I really like them. They don't try to act young like some of the teachers and other kids' parents... they just act their age."

"That's hard for adults to do sometimes, because they don't want to get old," Paul laughed. "What are you and the boys, maybe your brothers, doing in your dreams?"

Pulling her hair back tight behind her ears and deftly flipping it into a loose knot, "Usually we are playing 'pirates' and robbing some people and rescuing nice people. We never rob the nice people. We would bury our treasures and draw maps... then try to find them again later... by exchanging maps.

"Quick, Uhara-san. Over there! Look at all the fish swimming in a circle!" She pointed to an eddy near the riverbank.

They both just watched for a while... speculated a little, but could not figure out the reason for the behavior. The sun made them all twinkle like silver in the clean water that reflected a blue sky. Soon they all just swam away in spontaneous syncopation. Pretty.

"Sometimes I think something like that is the story of my life," said Paul. "I have just been swimming around in circles and surviving in the river of life... except, I never knew which crowd I belonged in. The fish are lucky."

"I think we girls at *Brigadoon* are beginning to think that way too. Uhara-san, did I mention that in one of the dreams I think there was a message for me?"

"No, do you want to tell me about it?"

Lili looked pensive as she stared at the spot where the fish had been swimming. It was different, Paul thought, for her to be so quiet for such a long time. Was she afraid of something?

After a long silence, during which time she threw several rocks in the river, she finally answered, "I'm not sure I should. I have never told this one to anyone."

"Well, you certainly do not need to tell me. Why have you never told Su, ah, Grandmother Benjamin?"

"I don't know. There was something about it that scared me and I don't like to be scared... and I didn't want anyone to know I was scared. I just tried to forget it. Is it okay to be scared? Were you ever scared?"

"Of course I've been scared. Only liars say they are never scared... because they're scared to admit it. Maybe I can help you to understand and it won't scare you anymore. Then you can talk more objectively, er, openly about it."

"I want to tell someone about it and the Benjamins trust you in everything, so I thought I should tell you and see what you think... here it is. Promise you won't laugh?"

"I won't."

"Well, we were playing by a big river. I think it was much, much wider than this one, muddier and slower. The biggest boy was much older... maybe ten years. He was telling us a story that his (our?) mother had told him about seeing a man come down in a parachute during a thunderstorm. She never saw an airplane, but she watched and followed him. He wore funny clothes and she saw him steal some clothes from her family's yard where her mother had hung them to dry under a shed roof. He headed for the river and she never saw him again. The big boy said he was from another planet because of the funny clothes. One of the other boys said that was not true because some months later he heard some of their cousins found some funny clothes way down the river and were afraid to tell anyone because they were made in America and their parents might get into trouble... so they buried them. The third boy said it was their duty to find the buried treasure." Lili stopped talking and looked at the river again.

"That was your dream?" Paul asked. He was stunned. Is it possible? He thought to himself... I guess it could be. Feeling a little rattled... he had to stop for a while. This was *not* what he'd expected.

"When the Benjamins told us some of your story, I thought I should start with that one, but there were more. Maybe I should tell them all to you before you think about them, so you can see if there's any connection that would tell me more about my family."

"Do you miss your family? Would you like to find them?"

"Not really. I don't think I ever really knew them. Grandmother and Grandfather have always loved me a lot since as far back as I can remember. I'm just curious."

"How much did the Benjamins tell you about me?"

"Grandpa told us you used to fly in the same squadron during your Air Force years and you spent many years in China... but he mostly talked about the airplane flying and how he enjoyed those days."

"He didn't tell you anything about my time in China?"

"No. He said if we ever met you, you could tell us that story if you wanted to. It happened so often that we got to that point... you can imagine how excited we were to hear you were coming! We're all curious.

Pebbles of JADE

Why were you living there? Tell us more about our homeland!"

"I'll tell you, but first, go on with your dream some more," said Paul... He needed a little time to think.

Closing her eyes, "Well, for some reason the boys in the dream agreed their mother was probably a bad lady because they remembered their father a little... and yet he was no longer around and they became very poor. Now that they were older, they realized he was not Chinese. They saw a picture of him once and he was dark skinned with a heavy black moustache. Their mother said she had been given to him when she was a little girl working at a big factory making drilling equipment. They said she called him her 'oil-man' and one day he, all of a sudden, had to go home... far to the west. They said she got really sick and died not long after that and they were sad, but got tired of taking care of her so they got their auntie down the river to help. One of them said to me in the dream that he would leave me someone or something that would help me learn more about where I was born and what my mother was like. The oldest boy said she was working in a big city at the end of the river on the coast and she would help get me *'re-connected to family'* through the Japanese. That was the end of that dream."

She started leading him up the riverbank again, kicking sand with every other step. Her serious face had its effect on Paul.

"I remember growing up with a sister and soon coming to a big house where I remember only a little bit of one conversation between some adults about me.

Someone asked if I should 'please men, or please women.' The argument stopped when someone else in the room said *'she should please God'* and she remembered thinking she did not know what *God* was. Then she remembered some long airplane rides... and she was here at Brigadoon. The only thing she remembered *always* having with her was one small little stuffed Chinese girl doll her mother had given her."

"Do you still have it?"

"That is what started my dreams."

"A doll?"

"One night, while going to sleep, I was holding it up to my face and I felt a knot in a thread between its legs. At first I thought nothing of it. But then I noticed it felt different than the other knots. I couldn't sleep... so I went into the bathroom and turned the light on. The thread was a little different color. I knew I could fix it again, so I opened the medicine cabinet and got out the little scissors and cut the knot... I was curious. As I opened up the doll a little, I found a piece of cotton cloth rolled up inside the stuffing. It had a map-like drawing on it and some Arabic numbers. I have been having dreams ever since."

"Have you figured it out?"

"A little bit. It shows a top northern loop in a river with three cities... I think it is the Yangtze, or Changjiang, and the tri-cities area I have found on a map in the southeastern part of Hupeh Province. I heard a man from there speak once and his dialect was different than Mandarin, and much different than

Cantonese. What most interested me was that I could understand him. When I get older I want to study oil-drilling, because I think that will help me understand what the numbers mean."

"Hmmm."

"In one of my dreams one of the boys, the middle one, said 'Look for the one man, the father of two. Both have white beards and should be enemies. From your new home, look to the east, it will be a new thing.' The other two boys vanished when he said that, yet this one was glowing and bright. Then he sort of disappeared in a fog, or a cloud. I have never understood any of that."

Kind of looking all around at *nothing* she continued, "The dreams I have had from then on have made no sense at all and were not fun anymore, so I haven't been telling them to Grandma anymore. The big city to the east at the end of the Yangtze River is Shanghai, but their dialect is different. Nothing in the dreams ever even looked familiar until we started studying social studies in school and I saw people dressed like those in my dreams. They were in the Middle East! They looked like Israelis and Arabs... Semitic! But, one of them did call himself a Hamite... whatever that is. Now I am really confused.

"Does this make any sense? Do you see why I can't tell anyone? They'll laugh at me and call me stupid or crazy."

"Would the Benjamins do that?"

"No, but I don't want them to even *think* that."

"Hmmm."

"Quit twirling your little beard. It makes you look like a mountain goat."

"Is that like a Pauly goat?"

"What's that?"

"Never mind," Paul chuckled. "Have *you* any ideas about what your dreams mean?"

Lili looked back at the river... her eyes glistening. "No... but I want some. I think they are important and they kind of scare me."

"Let's walk a little further up the river. I need to think a little. I don't have any good ideas at the moment either."

They walked silently for about ten minutes. Then, Paul stopped and put his hand on Lili's shoulder. As she looked up at him he said, "This is no good. I have no idea of where to begin interpreting your dreams. If it is any consolation to you, I had dreams during my years living in China, which I could never figure out either. However, when the 'almost war' happened some years ago right on the heels of that terrible terrorist attack in New York City and the ensuing years of working with other nations to route out terrorism... some things seemed as if I had thought of them before and was remembering them. I knew it had not happened before... so it was really a weird sensation. I think it had something to do with my dreams. Maybe that is happening to you. Maybe something big is about to happen. Without 'time' factored in, it's hard to sequence things out in ways that make sense. One would have to be *outside* of 'time' to see the big picture. I don't think we can do that."

"No, I don't think so either. How long were you living in China, Uhara-san?"

"Just under forty years."

"Forty years! You must really be old. When you had dreams, was anyone able to help you understand? Did they look at tea leaves and stuff?"

"No, I was like you… afraid to tell anyone because they would think me 'nuts' and it would draw attention to me. I only had them three times and they were always the same. Now I can't remember them. The good thing at the time was an old lady I had helped took me in and let me live in her home. She was new to Shanghai and was considered an outsider because she spoke a different dialect. Then I met my wife who moved in also and I never had any more dreams."

"You can't remember them! Why? Why were you afraid of *attention*?"

"I wasn't supposed to be there."

"Were you a spy?"

"No."

"Why didn't you come back home?"

"I couldn't without attracting attention. Then after a few years when I got a wife, we just settled into living out our life there… in this lady's home. A few years later the nice old lady we called 'mama' died and her place became ours. Nobody said anything. Once when we told her we couldn't have any children, she told us not to worry about it… they gave her the same operation. She secretly already had many more than she was supposed to, three boys and a girl who were all taken away from her. She never knew what happened to them because they also sent her away to work in Shanghai. That caused me to think about my life in America. I had no family, so I had nothing, really, to come back to."

"Then... why did you come back?"

"My wife died, I was alone again and I started remembering things. I was still an American. By then I knew a way to get out... so I did it and here I am. That's how I got to know Su-mei... none of you have heard that story yet."

"Will we?"

"I think so... oh, yeah."

"And is that when you met Grandfather Benjamin?"

"No. I knew him from before, remember? We still have some catching up to do."

Now it was Lili's turn and she asked, "Why do you think you had your dreams?"

"I often wondered that myself. After all those terrorist things happened a few years ago and I found I could not remember them... except that I had them... I finally decided they must have been some kind of preparation for me."

"How could that be? What could cause that? How would that be possible? Why?"

Paul rolled his eyes and chuckled, "Your guess is as good as mine. I don't know. Maybe someday we'll find out. Then maybe you too will have some answers to your dreams."

"When will that be?"

Pebbles of JADE

"Well, here's a clue. I'll tell you a little something right now so you won't be surprised when I tell more of the story to others."

She just stopped walking and sat down, crossed her legs with her elbows on her knees and her face in her hands looking up at Paul.

Laughing, "I guess it must be story time. Look, this is not going to take long, so don't get too comfortable. It's just that I think the person coming down in the parachute your mother saw... was me. This is an incredible coincidence. The place you saw on the little map in your doll sounds like the hump in the river west of what is on maps as Hanzhou in the southern part of the misty peaks of Huangshan Mountain where I ejected. Evidently I just missed seeing that beautiful area written of by the famous poet Li Bai. That must be near where you and your family were from. I was not in a mountain climbing mood at that time... just wanted to stay alive. All I could think to do was get down-river through the gorges to the east coast... and somehow get out of China.

"Do you think you met my mother?"

"It's very possible that I may have even lived in her home... I don't know. Time will tell... nothing would surprise me now. Maybe the best advice I can give you is to have patience... and just ponder your dreams in your heart without letting them worry you."

"That doesn't help much, but if that's what you did, Uhara-san, I guess that's all I can do." Reaching and grabbing his hand as he pulled her up she continued, "Thank you. It does help a little just knowing you went

BenOHADI

through something... maybe even near where I did. In fact, maybe it helps a lot!"

"I'm sorry I can't do more... not yet anyway. Maybe when I tell all of you about how I got to China in the first place it will help us understand. I think part of your dream was telling you a little about me. We'll see. What's puzzling is, why did I hear about this now?"

"Well, that will be interesting, but I don't know. Maybe I just needed to talk about it with someone and I did not know who it should be. I trusted you and you are a good listener... just as the Benjamin's said you would be. Thank you. Wouldn't that be awesome if you actually knew my mother? Now I have more to think about. Lets head back."

"Are you ready? Do you have more to tell me?"

"Yes. But it can wait and I want to just be by myself to think about my dreams some more. I think I am forgetting something. When I think of it I'll tell you. Please don't tell anyone about this."

"I won't." Now Paul was kicking sand and gravel as they walked. "I'm getting tired of thinking about myself all the time. Maybe you're going through the same thing."

"Maybe. Maybe you should talk to 'the Sao'. I once heard her say she had dreams in the daytime."

"Who?"

"I'm sorry. I shouldn't call her that. The boys at school call Ling Sao 'the Sao' as a joke, because she is so beautiful. One of the guys in 4H said it was spelled differently. The Senior boys are always after her, especially the football team, but the Benjamins have both had many talks with her about boys... and she *hangs* with Elona Li, which is good."

"Does she handle that okay?"

"The dreams, or the boys?"

"The boys."

"Oh, yeah. She and one of the seniors, a boy she knows at the Shepherd's congregation we worship with, have made a deal. He's a tall, really well built guy... strong! His parents won't let him play football for some reason, so he's on the town's soccer team and does quite well, but he has to be careful because he grew so fast and there are lots on his team that are smaller than him... although most of them are also faster, so they make up for it. Anyway, they made this deal that they will be good friends, but no messing around."

"What else was in the deal?"

"Well, everyone thinks they're going with each other... and they do go to the dances together, but that's all. I think he really does like her a lot, but he's a nice guy and she just wants a casual 'bodyguard' when there are strangers around. She understands what she does to boys, so she works hard at just being 'sweet' and quiet in public, which is really hard for her. When you are smart, helping other kids with their homework is easy... and the kids like her. Ask her about her dreams. She must be like me, because she said she's never told anyone either... even though she wants to tell her friend, Elona Li, who keeps telling us to imagine our karate moves as if we're dreaming... and performing in a 'dream-world' for men. Then she always adds a little 'watch out' with a wink."

"I'll ask her. Are you sure I should? What if she doesn't bring it up?"

"She will. She first mentioned it when we heard you were coming. Ask her if she thinks her friend is having them... and if so, does it have to do with hanging around out here?"

"We'll see. Don't want you to get in trouble with her."

"Time will tell," Lili giggled and flashed her smile. "I won't."

She pulled Paul's hand as they climbed back up the embankment to the 'Jade House'... *Brigadoon*, as they referred to it. He felt good that she trusted him and seemed to be feeling better. Maybe all she needed was someone to tell her experience to. On the other hand, that business about her mother remembering someone coming down in a parachute was just too coincidental to ignore. The information was not of much importance to him, but it would help establish a significant relationship with at least one of the girls. And what was that business regarding the Middle East? "One man, the father of two who should be enemies"... and the two kind of fade into the past. Were they the shadows of something to come? Maybe the "ghosts of Christmas past... and Christmas present"? None of it made any sense. A lot of help he was... it was depressing to realize he was only kidding himself by thinking he could help someone. Was *this* the story of his life?

6

EXTREME DREAM

As they walked into the cool shade of the old train depot that was their home from the bright, hot back deck, Paul heard piano and violin practice going on simultaneously. As his eyes adjusted he saw two girls about ten or twelve very intensely practicing from their music books. Looking past them, through the open front door, he saw an old pickup parked in the driveway, but no one else seemed to be around. Lili vanished up the long stairway. The truck looked like an old forties-vintage Studebaker, so he stepped out to look at it... that is when he saw Ling Sao and what looked like an old cowboy sitting on the bench, quietly talking. She waved, then waved him over.

"Uhara-san, please let me introduce you to Mr. Owen Morgan, owner of the Morgan Ranch. Mr. Morgan, this is Col. Paul Uhara, a long time friend of Grandfather's and a more recent acquaintance of Grandmother."

Owen stood and they shook hands. Ling Sao pulled up a chair for Paul and they sat down together.

"Uhara-san, Mr. Morgan is a second generation owner. His father 'homesteaded' the land and never

BenOHADI

left Valley County after he settled here. He himself has left our valley only a few times. He is what we call an 'old timer' out here."

Owen really looked like a cowboy... well-worn jeans, a red flannel shirt with rolled up sleeves, a leather western hat and almost worn-out boots that looked as if they had lots of stories to tell. He had a contentedly happy face with lots of suntanned lines and moved his head and upper body in continual "aw-shucks" language.

"Fascinating. Mr. Morgan, I'll bet you have a lot of stories to tell about the changes you've seen in this country. I would love to learn more about the *real* 'old west' and the people who settled here."

"Col. Uhara, I go by Owen around here... except for with these girls."

"Please call me 'Paul'... and it's the same here," Paul laughed. "However, I do appreciate how these girls have been taught to respect their elders. By the way, Ling Sao, where are the Benjamins?"

"Oh, they're here somewhere. If you did not see them when you came through *Brigadoon*, they may be over at their place having their 'Saturday *summa-time suk-suk*' and will be back out in a short time."

"What's that?" asked Paul.

"We don't know for sure," she answered, smiling. "At first we all thought it had something to do with summer, but they refer to it in during the rest of the year also. Grandmother always giggles when she mentions it. Once she mentioned something about *maki-sushi*, but they're not really into making Japanese

Pebbles of JADE

food. I think they are just using some old Chinese slang for *taking a nap*."

"Oh," Paul said… smiling to himself as he recalled some slang from his Hawaiian upbringing. Owen looked puzzled and said he, too, was finding it necessary to take naps more often.

"Mr. Morgan has offered all the Junior-Class High School girls out here at *Brigadoon* jobs next summer on his ranch. What do you think, Uhara-san? Do you think it is a good idea? Would the Benjamins approve? We have chores to do here."

"I don't know, Ling Sao. You would have to ask them. Owen, what would they be doing for you? Would it be safe?"

"Well, first of all, we've done this a few times in years past… but just for a few days at a time and they slept in our living room. My wife and I have learned there will only be about three, maybe four of them available next year. So this time they could live with us in what used to be our own kid's bedrooms. My wife says that would be safe. We have six cowboys who work for us every summer and live in the bunkhouse. The jobs would be for all summer and include cooking, cleaning, helping with cleanup of winter *deadfall* and mending fences. We would keep them busy and teach them about the ranching business at the same time. There is plenty to do. My wife even says she would teach them to '*can*' the crop from our fruit-trees. We could sure use the help these days… it's hard to get since most of the Basque moved out of the territory,

BenOHADI

except for my wife… bless her heart. She's Basque, you know," he smiled as he pulled out his pipe.

"Uhara-san," interrupted Ling Sao. "I am very excited about this offer. Next year I will probably be 'Polly' and I know we would all like to learn more about the old American 'West'. Mr. Morgan has even told me he would teach all of us to ride horses and 'break us in' to assisting in the 'round-ups'. Doesn't that sound like fun? Please, would you talk to Grandmother and Grandfather for us?"

Paul envisioned her well-proportioned body bouncing in a saddle and began to worry about the "hired help"… that would be doing the same thing. "I don't know. Let me think about that a little."

Ling Sao saw him looking at her, smiled and answered, "I know what you are thinking. Don't worry, the Morgans promised one of them would always be with us."

Owen finished pressing down the tobacco in his pipe and chuckled while saying, "These guys all have wives and kids in town and they have all been with me for many years. They are also heavily bonded and I've had background-checks done on them by the Sheriff's Office. I know they'll be okay. My wife would have some pretty strict rules for the girls also, to keep them from doing stupid and naïve things."

("Summa-time suk-suk" Paul thought to himself. He knew Peter and Su-mei were not naïve. He didn't want to get involved in this decision, but he wanted to let the girls have adventure… and still be safe and

Pebbles of JADE

protected.) "Why do you want to be a *cowgirl*, anyway? Do you really think the others want to do that also?"

"Oh, yes they do! We all read some Louie L'Amour books and dream of the *Old West* we only heard about before. Now we are here and want to learn first-hand!"

"I assume they know Mr. Morgan pretty well?"

"Oh, yes. They are old friends."

"Ling Sao, you ask them yourself... please. Owen, you say you folks have some kids? Tell me about them... and what's this about *bonded* cowboys?" Paul just wanted to change the subject.

"Well, first of all, we have three kids. One's an architect in Boston and in the Massachusetts Air National Guard at Otis AFB out on Cape Cod. He's settled and starting a family. The other son is in the Air Force, stationed at Aviano Air Base in Italy. He just got married to a gal in his squadron and they've both settled on Air Force careers. Our daughter is twenty-nine, has never been married, but is about to be. She met an Active Duty Naval officer when he was home for his wife's funeral at her family's congregation in Boise a few years ago. He's about ten or eleven years older than she and his kids are all on their own... but they seem to be a good match with common interests. Only the circumstances of their meeting were sad. Our daughter had been working with his wife who had become her friend and confidant. They have been staying in touch through his parents."

"How did the guy's wife die?"

"An auto accident… rather unusual and tragic… she was so young and he only had a few more years to go."

"What does your daughter do?"

"She was a barber at the Gowen Field BX for many years… where the girls met. Then she went to FBI school and is now working out of the Southern Idaho Field Office."

Ling Sao jumped in saying "I met her and I really like her. She kind of reminds me of Grandmother, only younger. But, she is just as beautiful as I imagine Grandmother was when she was that age. I never could imagine why Grandmother waited so long to marry. But after talking to Mr. Morgan's daughter one day, I thing I am beginning to understand."

"You have quite a family," said Paul.

"Yes, we are very proud of them all… even though we worried a lot about our daughter. She seemed slow to mature, but in another way, she always seemed too old for her age. She's okay now. Life is good. We just want to do something for these girls before they leave Idaho and America… and we have only recently figured out what we *could* do."

"And the *bonded* cowboys? I've never heard of such a thing. Is that normal?"

"Oh, yeah. We thought that up ourselves. Seems to work pretty good. We worked it out with our liability insurance company. We pay our boys better than average, but they have to buy this *bond* and pay for it with deductions from their paychecks. We match the amount they pay in a fund that acts as a bonus they collect at the end of the season... just in time for Christmas."

"Doesn't that cost you a lot?"

"You'd think so, but our insurance company worked out a way where we save an equivalent amount in what our 'liability' costs us. It's a 'break-even' that makes things better for everyone."

Peter came walking out of the old house south of the depot building, running his fingers through his wet hair. He had obviously just taken a shower. "What a beautiful afternoon... Oh! Hi, Owen. When did you get here?"

Standing up and sticking out his hand, "Peter. How ya doin' guy? I got here 'bout an hour ago. Me and the Sao here, as the boys at school call her, been talkin' 'bout a proposition me and the missus have fer ya. Are ya ready?"

"Sure... shoot. Want a beer?"

"Naw, its too early and she'd smell ma breath and wonder what I been up to."

Paul was enjoying listening to this old guy. He was very articulate when he wanted to be, but he could also sound a real "country boy" when he had a mind to. He guessed that he had fooled more than a few with the "cowboy charm" of his voice and the easy smile he had on his wrinkled, leathery face as he ambled about on his saddle-bowed legs. So this was what Ling Sao had dreamt of!

"Whatcha got Owen?"

BenOHADI

"I been 'splainin' to the Sao here that me and the missus wants to hire a bunch of 'em to hep us next summer when the snow melts. Whadya think?"

"Ling Sao, is this your idea?"

"No, grandfather. Mr. Morgan came here to ask you."

"What do *you* think?"

"I think it would be marvelous! We would love to become 'cowgirls' and work on a real western ranch!"

"Chinese cowgirls. I can see the headlines now. They're underage, Owen, you know that. You talking about a few weekends or all summer?"

"They'd just be guests on our ranch, helping out with the chores. We'd contribute to *Jade West*, your non-profit organization. Affa thet you kin do whatcha want."

"Is that a bribe?" Peter laughed.

Owen pushed his weather-beaten old hat back on his head and said, "Course not! Just statin a 'fact of life' regardin them plans."

"Ling Sao, what about the gardening here... your chores during the summer?"

"I don't know, Grandfather. Please, can't we work something out?"

"I don't know, either, Ling Sao. Let me talk to the 'boss' about this and get back to you. Owen, can you stay for supper tonight? We're barbecuing some pork steaks and you're welcome."

"Pork steaks! I've got some *real* steaks on ice in the back of that there truck that I was just bringin' out to you folk as thet 'bribe' you wuz talkin' 'bout. Use some of them and I'll stay. We bred 'em lean so none a the older gals or your missus need worry."

Laughing, "Thanks, Owen. I think we just changed the menu. If you want to bring them into the kitchen, I'll help. Then I have another little project I could use some help with. Do you mind? Su-mei should be out any minute and we can talk about your '*proposition*'."

Looking serious again, "Ling Sao, you're too emotional about this. Why don't you take Uhara-san for a walk so we can talk alone a little… okay?"

"Yes, Grandfather," Ling Sao said, standing up and offering her hand to Paul.

Paul thought to himself, "Another walk? I'm too old for this," but Ling Sao was already pulling him back down the hill.

As they reached the riverbank and she started to lead Paul downstream she said, "I'm glad I was asked to do this. I have wanted to talk to you. I had this dream that has been bothering me and hope you can help. Grandmother said I should talk to you when you arrive."

"I think I know what it is."

"How? I have not told you yet."

"Well, you said you always dreamt of being a 'cowgirl', isn't that true?"

"Yes, but that is completely different. That was more of a *yearning*, this is different, this was a real dream I have had about once a week since I started becoming a woman."

"What?"

BenOHADI

"You know," she blushed. "Since I started menstruating. I was early. It started two years ago and then I started growing up here… you know."

Paul was old and thought it didn't happen anymore… but found himself blushing. "What's your dream?" he asked.

"Maybe I should begin with what I think may have triggered it in the first place."

"Go on."

"It was a rainy, dreary afternoon and I was standing in the Great Room, looking out the big window, wondering what to do with my time now that school was out and none of could do anything outdoors. I saw a small pile of magazines and noticed there had been a series of articles published about this Dr. Mandrake that everyone had been talking about. After sitting down to read them, I discovered they were consistent with everything I'd heard. He was a fascinating, riveting speaker and his personality was kind, merciful with many acts of goodness and intelligent. His perceived authority was rapidly growing.

Evidently, after so many years of tribulation in the Middle East, he had earned the trust of everyone. He's a problem-solver and seems to bring *peace*. Both the Jews *and* the Palestinians love him! Because of that, American Christian denominations of all sizes have paid great attention to him and support him financially. Even the new Pope for the Roman Catholics is encouraging his loyal subjects to help him politically because Dr. Mandrake has promoted the legitimacy of the Vatican in the ever more popular United Nations."

"Yeah. That's what I've been hearing too."

"Well, the next article went on to explain his problem-solving *vision* has shown his uncanny ability to forecast the outcome of proposed solutions and has earned him the reputation of being a *'miracle worker'* resolving some age-old battles. His obvious love for all humanity has even allowed for architects and engineers from around the world to work together in a U.N. committee for the restoration of Babylon and their world famous *hanging-gardens* to their former glory… and to also work together in rebuilding King Solomon's magnificent temple. Operating from his office in that custom furnished Boeing 7E7 he often serves as the communications center for U.N. peacekeeping efforts by quickly relocating his 'Restoration-Consensus' teams to wherever they're needed. The Islamic world is not complaining because he brought about a true, independent Palestinian State and the *old-guard* of the Israeli Government is gone… again, thanks to him. He's wonderful!"

"Be careful," Paul warned, but she continued…

"With so much cultural interaction under his leadership, international economic balance and success has never been better. Peace has pretty much come all over the world and, for the most part, his position is recognized as that of the 'Messiah' for the Jews, the 'Reconciler' for the Islamic and the 'Second Coming of Christ' to begin the 'Millennial Reign' of the world's king by the Christians.

"The last article talked about how five or six years ago we started hearing about these two guys making speeches *against* him all over the world... and they were remarkably good! Many of the Christian, or *Messianic* Jews started emigrating spreading their testimony... many, including Elona Li's family, to the U.S. They referred to it as *escaping* to warn others. When the Dome of the Rock was blown up a few years ago, those two guys were apprehended by a mob as the terrorist perpetrators, tortured, mutilated and beheaded in the marketplace of Jerusalem. More people emigrated. Remember all that?"

"Oh, yeah!"

"Remember what happened next and what debate it stimulated in the media?"

"Oh, yeah... where are you going with this?"

"Well, there are two men. One is from the desert area between Masada, in Israel, and the Dead Sea. The other is from Egypt. The first is a Christian Palestinian and the second a Coptic Christian. That seems to be the only thing they have in common, because they have difficulty nationalistically with each other, except for the beards and their faith in the God of Israel and His Messiah. Their dialects of Arabic are different. Well, maybe there is something else... they are both very vocal and charismatic speakers. They make lots of speeches to large crowds and are both making the news as very popular lecturers in various government agencies and universities... particularly among the Jews in Israel."

"Do they have a large political following?" asked Peter, wondering what this was all about.

Pebbles of JADE

"I don't know. But in the dream the news media seems to pay attention to them for several years for many reasons. Believe it or not, one of the things they've talked about is a 'peace' highway between Syria and Egypt. Wherever they go, which is always in an outdoor stadium, they always enjoy beautiful weather and a good turnout... even when the weather is really bad all around. They make lots of public speeches about religious beliefs... which is supposed to be illegal for them to do in their countries, because they are *against* Mandrake, who is beginning to be regarded as a god."

Paul was now connecting with her thoughts and jumped in, "The foreign news media is also becoming increasingly afraid of them because whenever someone speaks badly of them, something happens to that person and they die. Just as when Moses was trying to get the Israelites out of the clutches of the Pharaoh... usually of some disease, natural causes or in an accident... like in the ancient 'curses' and scary! Western reporters, broadcast and newspaper editors don't seem to like having to be so objective and non-editorial... and especially they don't want to be accused of being intimidated in such a spooky way. The phenomenon is something they cannot scientifically understand, deal with, or accept. They don't want to publish the speeches these guys make about the teachings of Christian's Jesus of Nazareth, whom they seem to regard as 'public enemy number one'... even though he was executed such a long time ago by *Pax Romana*, the justice of the Roman Empire."

Then trying to get her back to her dream he asked, "Is each dream showing you a little more, sequentially, yet always about the same subject?"

"Yes. I know none of this has anything to do with me... but because of the linkage of all these dreams, I think people should be afraid. I know I am. I just wish I knew 'of what'... because of what's happened in the Middle East, North Africa, South America and the big cities all over the world. I hear of terrible things happening to people who don't accept this *'Doctor's'* authority and control. We've kind of been immune from all of that way out here in the 'sticks' like they are in Asia. But aren't you a little afraid of what's going on... and that it might come to the rural areas also?"

"The dreams never show you what's happening?"

"No. And listening to other Christians in school, they say there is nothing to be afraid of because, if anything, this must be Christ whose come again because the *'Rapture'* has not yet happened to rescue us from the *'Tribulation'* of the Anti-Christ before the end. Something is wrong! I think we're in trouble already and this is what Elona's parents have been warning us about.

"In fact, in the last dream the two guys are together... in front of the Wailing Wall in Jerusalem. The one named Elias invoked God to cause a severe drought and turned the water produced by Mandrake to alleviate it into blood. Then they caused different plagues to occur to those who talked about the *'Doctor'* as a god. I've just overheard one of the parents that comes out here that he was in a central part of the temple being rebuilt and told the press he *was* god... with a big, friendly smile on his face. They were interviewing him just after some major catastrophe... and the dream made it clear the meeting had been arranged by someone that controls the air, yet lives in the earth."

"*In* the earth... like in caves?"

"Yes! Not on the earth and not in caves, but *in* the earth somehow... with influence everywhere."

"And what... he has an airborne command post or something?"

"I know it sounds crazy, but I guess that's how dreams are. It is like this thing was *part* of the air and the earth itself and it arranged that these two guys should finally come to him. At first they are looking out from the very high windows of a restaurant that seemed to overlook the world and they agree to meet again in King David's great city and take on Mandrake face to face. They just make it out when suddenly and angrily the great building they were in is attacked from the air by killers that had no regard for human life... all under the guidance of that *power*. Many innocent people, who thought they were so safe inside, suddenly found their building violently penetrated and their lives mercilessly, sometimes painfully extinguished. Instantly their first meeting place turned into, like, an inferno. And just as quickly, everyone in the great international city mourned their death over the two tombstones that were at first seen and then vanished. Later it was discovered and reported that the two *'olive branches'*, as the media liked to facetiously refer to these two who were speaking out against the world's new man of peace, Doctor Mandrake, had shown up in Jerusalem."

Her hands moved as if she was throwing a ball from one to the other. "The next thing I see are their dead and mutilated bodies on a Jerusalem street, and the Dome of the Rock is in the background... a smoldering pile of rubble! Uhara-san, I am mostly puzzled by what everything might mean... and just a little scared. Can you help? Does any of this make sense?"

"Ling Sao, I don't know... probably not." Here I go again, he thought to himself. "Is that it? When did you have these dreams... at night or during the day? And, was that your last dream?"

"Yes, that was the last dream. They started out just being early morning dreams. Then I started getting them when I would lie down on the grass to take naps or watch clouds in the sunlight while out on walks through the fields around here... that was just this summer. I have been having them for a little over three years. Only in the last few months did I start getting scared, because more kept being added to them. And there's one last thing."

"Well, as I'm sure you are aware from the news of a few years ago, the mosque in Jerusalem was destroyed and two guys caught in the street were mobbed, tortured, mutilated, killed and beheaded... accused of being the terrorists that did it. That guy curiously named *Mandrake* led the mob and insisted their bodies be left in the street to rot... as an example. Since then he has established quite a reputation for himself, causing many Jews to claim him as their 'Messiah' and many Christians in America to see him as Christ returning to establish his kingdom. A remnant of Jews who became Christians after listening to the two men have fled, presumably in fear of impending danger they've heard of. But, many other Christians have been saying the only 'danger to come' is the *Tribulation* to be experienced by those who don't worship the *returned* Messiah… Mandrake!"

"Yes, I knew about all of that because that was when Elona's family arrived here. Her parents emphatically warned us against that man, saying he was evil… even though lots of churches all over were really becoming alive and financially successful while planning many pilgrimage tours over there, often as volunteer labor to help Mandrake in the Temple project. Believe me, her family was *adamant* we 'stay the course'…and stay away! We did."

"Was there anything unusual about this last one compared to the others?"

"Two things. Mr. Morgan has been letting me ride one of his horses. I found a trail up West Mountain that was kind of gentle on Magnum, the horse, then found a really private spot with a big flat rock that faced the afternoon sun… away from the lake. Whenever I was off Magnum I noticed she was excellent about letting me know if someone was approaching. Don't you *ever* tell the Benjamins, but three days ago I was up there and was feeling pretty bold and the rock felt so nice and cool in the hot sun, so I took off all my clothes and sunbathed for a while on it. I was stretched out on my back and it felt so good. I was not really asleep, when I had that last dream. It startled me and... this is really strange... I was thinking of the emergency phone number 'nine-one-one'! I had a cellular phone with me, but could not figure out what emergency I would be calling in for. Nothing was wrong. Then, before I got dressed I had an 'awake' dream, for the first time. I was kind of looking at the sun and saw the two men arising from the rubble... only now the scene was back in Jerusalem again and their bodies had been dead in the street for over three days. They were recognized and huge crowds gathered to see! They were alive! Then they just sort of floated up with the smoke from the smoldering fires and steam and vanished. I finished dressing and came home. You're the first person I have told this to."

"Ling Sao..."

"You think I'm crazy, don't you?"

"No, but I don't know what to think. I won't tell anyone about our conversation, but I do need to think about it a little. I don't have any good ideas... except, that '911' thing."

Looking down at his trembling hands, "If I recall, a year before the '*almost war*', when those airplanes ran into the World Trade Center, the date was September 11th. The news often referred to it as '*9-11*'. During the next few years it was on various internet news sites that there were huge numbers of people quietly defecting from Islam and Zionist Judaism. Some were speculating it was because of two very popular public speakers who had been roaming the Middle East

Pebbles of JADE

separately, who were in a lot of political trouble. I wonder… It really was curious that so many Arabic countries had started to become openly friendly with the U.S. after that attack and did not jump at the chance to invade when the U.S. was attacked again, and was so vulnerable, by the People's Liberation Army of Communist China years later."

Holding out his trembling hands and continuing, "You're so right, Ling Sao. Look at this. I can feel it in my bones. This *is* really weird. Now I am curious to learn more about what was going on in the Middle East when all that stuff started happening here in America and over in China. Whooee! I've had enough for one day. I'm ready for another Guinness. Let's go back. What made you think *I* would understand any of this? All you've done is make me take a harder look at current events."

"When we get back," Ling Sao said, looking down and smiling, "you stay down on the benches by the river and I'll go get the beer for you. The benches are pretty much out of sight of everyone and that way I can have one with you."

"You're bad!"

"I am not! But it wouldn't be right for you to get *me* one and I've only done this once before… when I started my period. Please!"

Paul smiled and said. "Okay, scratch out everything that we just now said so's I can stay innocent. Let's start over, I'll repeat myself… Ling Sao, I'm tired. When we get to the benches I'd like to sit and rest a little. Would you please run up and get me a beer? The sun feels so good."

"Yes, Uhara-san. It would give me great satisfaction to please such an honored guest," she giggled in a low voice. She was really different he thought to himself.

SEVENTH TENET OF FAITH

Listening to the river while watching as if hypnotized, silently finishing about half their beers, Paul subconsciously determined he should lighten up the conversation they'd had earlier by changing the subject. He wanted to do some research, beginning with finding out what Peter and Su-mei might know. Had something recently happened he was unaware of?

He held up his bottle and said, making a 'toast', "Here's to womanhood." She clinked her bottle to his and he continued, "How does it feel?"

"I don't know," she smiled weakly. "But, I'm sure it feels good. Someday I'll find out, but I'm determined to be patient and don't want to rush it and ruin it."

She caught him off guard and he blushed again. That wasn't what he was asking and he felt awkward as he *raced* in his mind for an appropriate response.

"Good for you. You'll be quite a catch for some young man," he smiled and tapped her shoulder with his bottle.

"Thank you. I'll bet your Yulin thinks you to be one too."

"Thank you! I hope so. I'll find out soon, when I get back out there."

"When I was inside getting these, there were a lot of my sisters already back. They asked about you because they all want to talk to you. I told them I would bring you back soon, so I guess we better get back."

Paul chugged his beer and noticed Ling Sao pour about half of hers out. She handed her bottle to him and as they reached the deck at the top of the embankment she pointed to the trash can. Several of the girls immediately crowded around him and Ling Sao suggested he stay out on the deck with them and she would get him another Guinness if he thought three would not be too many. "You're generous... Please," he replied. "It's good they're the small ones." How could such a little girl have such a husky giggle? Must be that Russian blood, he thought.

The rest of the day, through a lively dinner and into the evening, Paul told stories about everyday life in China, answering all their questions as fast as they came at him. They wanted to know who they were and he was proving to be their best source of information regarding ordinary Chinese life. They were fascinated, while he became reflective...

The people were not the problem... it was the ideology of the elitists, most of whom were now gone because of Islamic suicide bombers and civil war, and because of what the Chinese Communist Party did to themselves in a desperate move a couple years back. After the "Manhattan Massacre," the attack against the U.S. Military at the Pentagon and the ensuing "War on Terror" involving many years and many countries, they still had almost managed to start WW-III with their surprise move from the Far East... creating an additional *Western Front* for America. It seemed that now the news from around the world was daily exposing some new tribulation for people somewhere insanely bent on control and death. When would it end? The long question and answer period that exercised his mind in many directions and caused him to remember and reflect on so much had left him feeling gratified, but whipped. When he finally *hit the sack,* he opened the window by his bed a few inches for some fresh Idaho mountain air, remembered to pull a comforter over himself, *crashed* and slept like a baby.

In the cool Sunday morning sunrise he sweat through a surreal, 'eleventh-hour' dream... about Islam and what had recently, so typically, *leaked out* and was becoming known in the media as the "Seventh Tenet of Faith" after *Jihad*. In the dream he was an invisible observer at a meeting of Muslim clerics that declared Afghanistan's old, and overthrown, Taliban government was contrary to the Talmud's teaching about the Cherisher of Mankind... This was nothing new to the Shi'a and the Sunni these days. However, what happened next was. Muhammed himself had, evidently, appeared to all of those in attendance in their own dreams with the same message to each. They had all been instructed to write, as they were just now learning, what turned out to be the *same* message. They all produced what they had fearfully written and brought with them in cloth wraps, so they would not touch them. All were reluctant to show what they had written:

"Zionism is wrong, causing those involved to worship themselves as *atheists* do. All violence is wrong because it uses human hands to work

BenOHADI

the evil mischief of Darkness over all of God's created things. The eternal proclamation of the God, before being born as the human, Jesus the Nazarene, Mary's son, and epitomizing *Mankind* and *Shang-ti*'s acceptable sacrifice for all sin, always was the very Voice, or Word of the only real God. I (Muhammed) was sent to bring unity, but instead, I heard and listened to a *whisper* behind me. Now I know all... and I am doomed. I was outside of time when I spoke to Lazarus who preceded me. Now in the God's wisdom and mercy I have been allowed to complete my message to mankind among the Jinns for protection. When questioned on that Day of Judgment, the Thamud must know and you must tell them. I became Zamil on a field of research with Uzair for the Lord and Cherisher of Mankind. I invented the name *Allah* as purification into *one*, out of the many Persian demonic gods, particularly Ormuzd (principle of good) and Ahriman (principle of evil). They had become systematically important in the Persian Empire... as the *Yin-Yang* of the East had become. Regardless of how men might attempt to refashion YHWH, the only true God, in the image of themselves, He still is Most Gracious, Most Merciful and did send to **all** *of mankind from their first delivery into the world,* His Redeemer... whom the Jews and Greeks called Messiah and Christ. I am sent under the unusual command of the merciful and gracious God of the Universe from the judgement of the dead as the last messenger... which I deceptively tried to do once before in human history, causing the loss of many eternal souls. **Have faith in Yeshua's message of love alone. Listen!**"

There was a great uproar and many crumpled the paper they had written or pushed it away as something untouchable with shaking hands. When someone inspected the papers and it was realized they had all recorded the same message in almost exactly the same words... and what had just happened as they gathered and made the comparison, several passed out... the rest just sat in shock, not knowing what to do. Curiosity became *fear*.

Paul awoke trembling.

BenOHADI

7

ULTIMATE THINGS

Paul dressed quickly in slacks, open shirt and a tweed jacket... perfect for going out with them this morning to wherever it was they went to church... it didn't make any difference where. All he could think about this morning was *God!* This had never happened to him before. He felt overdressed for going to breakfast, so he hung his jacket by the door. This was certainly different for him. He usually slept in on Sunday mornings, then went out for breakfast and the Sunday paper. There was only one girl in the kitchen, but he could hear lots of 'girl-noises' upstairs. He smiled to himself and thought how girls 'getting ready' for anything probably sounded the same... all over the world. He got his coffee, but was glad they were so busy when they started coming downstairs because he was still bothered by the dream and really did not feel like talking to anyone. After a little to eat he grabbed his jacket and went out on the deck to drink more coffee and just watch the morning sun first create fog, then slowly thicken it over the river before it started to burn it off. The air was clear and crisp. The morning colors were almost breathtaking against the backdrop of the little mountain range that rose to eighty-five hundred feet.

They all traveled to town in their two vans driven by Peter and Su-mei. He found out that three of the girls had driver's licenses, but were allowed very limited driving privileges. Where they worshipped was a classic old building that had evidently been remodeled a few times. He knew there were others, but this seemed to be the most obvious *Church* in town with its tall, white steeple. As they went in he noticed the huge stained glass depicting a shepherd and the round window above very inviting heavy, solid, beautiful front doors... both were swung open wide in an inviting way. There was a sign to one side saying, *"Welcome to the Shepherd's Chapel."* The cornerstone had written in three lines: *"1905 Thunder City - St. John the Forerunner - Shepherd of the Mountains 1980".* Maybe someone could explain that to him later.

Passing through the *narthex*, everything seemed very traditional in décor, with three gothic-arched stained-glass windows down each side of the sanctuary depicting the Creation Story. Where they would worship was a very white, cathedral ceiling room with a little gold-gilt symbolism here and there, plus some colorful banners and a lot of pews instead of chairs. It reminded him of where he would go with his parents as a boy in Hawaii... especially with all these oriental girls running around! What was it called? "Good Shepherd"... on Kuakini Street in Honolulu?

Many of the girls introduced him to many of their friends, mostly girls... and he realized just how

Pebbles of JADE

international the place seemed with the mingling of Asians, Latinos and Caucasians... some were even Basque. What a beautiful mixture of features: high cheekbones and slanted green eyes and brows, thin straight and pulled-back hair; or, large brown eyes with thick and cascading dark hair; or, very light skin with blond, red or brown hair of various lengths and blue, brown or hazel eyes. A few of the really blond girls had let their hair grow long, also... and there was a range of heights from very tall to very short. None seemed to indicate any weight problems. Either they were all very athletic, or diets must have improved immensely in recent years. They seemed to exhibit the full spectrum of healthy femininity and there must have been one to two dozen of them. Incredible.

The bulletin he was handed indicated this was the early service with fellowship and classes afterward. As the service began, he was pleasantly surprised at just how good the hymn-singing sounded to the accompaniment of the piano. The accompaniment was not at all overpowering. Looking back and up into the balcony he noticed the organ had a cover over it... must only be for special occasions. Then he was in for a bigger surprise. He soon figured out this was a congregation that used *liturgy*, which he had not been around for *ages*.

He didn't go to church, but he always thought nobody liked old-fashioned liturgy, so he didn't even try. He listened. What's this? No piano? They were simply all singing and glancing in their books very infrequently... some had their eyes closed. They

BenOHADI

seemed to know it by heart! The pastor would start something and they would flow into a response very smoothly... then he would kind-of flow back in. There did not seem to be any 'starting' and 'stopping'... it all sort of slowly and harmoniously overlapped. And there was no accompaniment! And... sometimes they were singing in harmony! It was magnificent! It made him kind of *melt* inside. He had no idea this old-style traditional liturgical worship could be so beautiful. In his youth it had always seemed so stilted, rushed and just repetitious to him... was he really in the Heartland of Idaho, the remnant of the old American West?

Not too many years ago he did some personal research by visiting a few churches on the West Coast, shortly after he'd smuggled himself back into the U.S. All the American Evangelical congregations were either shallow in a politically correct sort of way, or pseudo-intellectual without much historical Church knowledge. They liked to sing *syrupy* or up-beat songs while clapping and then clap more for their own performance... which seemed ridiculous. Sometimes they were more like entertainment concerts to make people happy. Presbyterians had about the same theological spin with more of the larger, denominational flavor. Roman Catholic services, on the other hand, had an equal degree of congregational involvement, but their singing was pathetic. The Episcopals only seemed to be trying to *out-catholic* the Romans. And the Lutherans were divided between the pure-doctrine preservers and the mission-minded. The one thing the last group had in common was they were well educated without being snooty and could sing very well. But, their liturgy was some kind of staccato-stilted leftover from their German heritage, or they abandoned it entirely in a poor imitation of American Evangelicalism... and calling themselves *Lutheran* only seemed to confuse outsiders, thwarting their mission efforts. Too bad five hundred years ago they were so ethnocentric and did not simply re-identify themselves as the German-Orthodox. Of course, what would they have called themselves when they came to America?

Then he noticed three of the Jade-girls and four other women who were together on one side in the back functioning as sort of a little liturgical choir... but, he also noticed they were not the only ones singing in *parts*. They were just leading the responses and all over the congregation different people were singing parts *with* them. He felt he was sitting in the middle of a gentle choir... found himself closing his eyes and again 'melting' to their voices in worship directed in focused attention to the altar with an unwrapped burial cloth across it and cross-shaped resurrected-Christ suspended above.

The pastor was a muscular, happy man who looked like an ex-Marine that needed no microphone. His sermon was no book-report, lecture or speech... more of a Bible-study focused on the lengthy Scripture readings that had preceded it. Obviously, he was a well educated theologian.

An hour and ten minutes after first walking in, their one hour of public worship was over for the week and they were in the parish's 'fellowship hall' drinking

BenOHADI

coffee or tea again... and digging into assorted refreshments. After about fifteen minutes, the girls all divided up into several classes, mostly upstairs, and Paul stayed with Peter and Su-mei who met with the pastor's group.

The class was in the midst of studying all the passages in the Bible that dealt with descriptions of the "Kingdom of God" and "Heaven." Su-mei was very involved because, she said, Chinese culture has always had much interest in "Heaven and Christ the eternal Tao." Paul just listened. He didn't know much about anything they were talking about... and his dream still bothered him. He would tell Peter and Su-mei about it later. For the moment, there seemed too much to listen to and learn and he had never felt so *disinclined* to debate. It seemed time to listen, discuss and maybe learn something.

When they finally returned to *Brigadoon*, the girls quickly dressed down a little, some completely changed, and were setting up a brunch on the deck overlooking the river and the mountains. It was a beautiful day. And soon they were back to questions and answers... only this time Paul was less animated and more quiet. The girls started to notice... and began asking if he felt okay. He did need to talk about his dream, but knew they would not understand a great deal about Middle-Eastern religion and politics... had Peter and Su-mei kept up? In his childhood he had a few dreams, but never in his life had he experienced a dream that seemed so real... and he was trembling inside again. He also was beginning to feel a strong

Pebbles of JADE

urge to return to Yulin and old Pirate Pete out in the Pacific. There was something he *had* to tell them and he couldn't put his finger on what it was or why he was in a hurry.

The rest of the day was deliciously pleasant, listening to the girls go through their *Tamarac Sisters* routines as they practiced… and just casually discussing everything these cute little Asian beauties wanted to talk about. They were fun and seemed to accept his reticence as just an indication of his age. Getting tired *did* make him feel old. He let them think that way about him, because they were partially right.

That night, as the younger ones were going to bed a little earlier because of school in the morning, he went south on a walk alone down along the top of the river embankment. It was through pastureland overlooking the river with the mountains in the background silhouetted against the indigo-blue of an early night sky. While crossing a fence he saw *Polly* running to catch up with him, so he stopped and waited.

"Elizabeth Jade Star is your full name, right?"

"Yes," she panted, let out a "*whoosh*" and said… "Do you mind if I walk with you? I need a little advice and I am sensing I better do it sooner rather than later because I don't know how long you are staying with us. Do you mind?"

"Of course not. What's on your mind."

The moon was just bright enough that they had no difficulty walking, but it was beginning to get very cool… almost cold. Paul was glad he had put his lined

BenOHADI

jacket on and noticed Elizabeth also wore a heavy wool sweater.

"Well, I graduate from high school this year," she began. "I will be flying to Shanghai and then on to Guling in a small sea-airplane. Someone will meet me from *Jade Far East* when I arrive."

"Flying has become quite expensive since all of the terrorist activity of the last few years. I'm glad the Benjamins have those expenses under control. Are you excited? That should be a very different adventure for you."

"Yes, I am excited... and yes, I found out how much they were spending for tickets and you are right. It's *really* expensive! But that is not my concern, although I *do* appreciate it. I look forward to my year working up there in the cool mountains, learning more of the language and learning a lot more about Chinese history and culture. They have survived so many trials! I also have been looking forward to the *Seer School* across the valley. We have been corresponding and they have been instructing me on how to *continuously* pray. I have been trying, but something has started happening that is confusing me. I never had dreams before and now I see these little images every morning when I awake."

Softly, almost to himself, "Oh, no. Not more dreams."

She seemed to read his mind, smiled, then quickly turned serious.

"Well, no, they're not really dreams I don't think. It's just like seeing glimpses of an old silent movie, but nothing seems familiar. Yet… they give me the feeling I am at home. At first I thought I was dreaming of life at Shangri-la…"

"Shangri-la?"

"Oh, not the Shangri-la of the old *Lost Horizon* movie," she giggled. "This is what *Jairus' Daughter's* call *Jade Far East*, just as we call our *Jade West* 'Brigadoon'."

Paul held a couple strands of barbed wire apart so she could get through a fence, then she reciprocated and they continued down the path.

"Go on."

"The people I was seeing did not look Chinese. I suppose a few did… a little. But there was a real variety of different features and all looked much healthier than me."

"Well, you look pretty healthy."

"Not next to them! I looked small and anemic as I stood next to them."

"You could see yourself in your dream?"

"I told you, it did not seem like a dream, as others have described dreams to me. And yes, I could see myself. I was the only one wearing clothes and was able to walk around and look at things… didn't just see things happen, like dreams."

"What!" Paul stopped walking and just looked at her. "You had a 'vision', that was *not* a dream, of an international nudist camp?"

"No!" she squealed. "They were not nude!"

"But you just said…"

BenOHADI

"I said they wore no clothes that I could see, and I could see the features of their bodies... sort of. But they seemed to have sort-of something all around them like protective, thick air."

"Thick hair?"

"No. *Air!*" she giggled. "I also could not tell the males from the females, even though they all had very distinctive features, different hair and physiques... even different faces and eyes. They seemed very confident, not embarrassed or weak at all... and didn't seem to be either male *or* female. It was like they all looked like *both*... sort of. I don't know!"

Paul laughed a little and said, "Shouldn't be too hard to recognize men from women, if they had no clothes on!"

"Don't laugh. It was. I could not see anything "down there" on any of them... if they were different sexes. They almost looked like a combination of a man and a woman, except for what I couldn't see. There did not seem to be any 'couples' even though some of them looked pregnant and they all seemed very happy. The glimpse I get each morning is different and does not last long after I start to move around in them."

Paul thought of his own dream and asked, "Is it scary? Or does it make you feel uneasy about all the evil going on in the world?"

"Not at all! I felt like I was not even in this world, yet at home. For some reason I wanted to stay with them... but it didn't feel like it was the right time yet. Really strange. Does this have anything to do with my trip to China? Did you ever see anything like what I've just described over there?"

"No." He though of an old movie before her time... was it "Contact"?

"Why do I keep dreaming about it then? What am I seeing?"

"Do you read 'science fiction'? I guarantee you, males and females are no different in China than they are here... that way."

"Hmm. I didn't read much when I was little in China. But a few years ago, for school, I read some Jules Verne, Ray Bradbury, and C.S. Lewis. Nothing lately, why? Do you think I'm dreaming 'science fiction'?"

"It was just a thought."

"I don't usually think much about space-travel and stuff like that. But I did once wonder whether it might be possible for there to be mechanical devices in the spiritual world... such as with UFOs, etc."

"What did you decide?"

"That if they could interact in our physical world, surely they could invent and use mechanical devices. Unless they were not very smart, stupid or unprepared. I remember wondering how, in the UFO stories, they could move so fast in one direction and then so suddenly change directions. Wouldn't they experience physically impossible *g-forces*?"

"Never thought about that. I once wondered if they would be good people or bad?"

"Either way," she went on, "they would first try to use humans for their work. If that did not work well, only then would they try to do things themselves. They might even try to make some humans of their own, if they could, like God did. But I doubt they would be very good at it. I thought about that after one of my dreams. All the people I saw were very *different* in appearance. They did not all have the same build, features, color and shape of eyes, or even the same kind of hair... they had glorious hair. They did *not* look like pictures of *aliens* with big, bald heads, huge vacant eyes and skinny bodies."

"Oh, yeah," she continued. "I did see some machinery. It was moving dirt and hauling materials. I remember looking at it because both the little stuff and the big stuff worked so well, so fast... and so quietly. I also saw people in some open, convertible-like cars and they were visiting. I did not see anyone just driving around by themselves in cars like we do... and one time I just saw someone kind-of 'materialize' in front of me. Several times I noticed people that I had not been watching sort-of just vanished. No one seemed bothered by any of this. And then! Get this... I saw a bunch of younger ones actually 'racing' in some little things, none of them looked exactly the same, sort of like those 'scooters' in the *Star Wars* movies. It looked like a bunch of boys, or girls, I could never figure out which. The adults around just watched, smiled... and I could have sworn I saw one of them mouth the word: 'kids'... but I never *heard* anything and don't know what language they used. I even saw babies and I'm sure I could tell what they were thinking... just a little, anyway."

Pebbles of JADE

"How many of these dreams did you have?"

"I told you, I don't think they were dreams because they just seemed to be 'snatches of some other life, somewhere. Lots. At least twenty-five... no, maybe as many as fifty over the years since I started, you know, thinking and praying about the *Seer School*. That's why I want to go there."

Paul had never heard so much talk about *"dreaming,"* even though that was not what she wanted to call it. What had he gotten himself into? Peter and Su-mei never talked about this. Why were all these kids having dreams? Why did *he* have one... and what did *it* mean?

First a little girl is meeting with what might be a couple of her brothers in China, when she was really young, as if she was going back in time, and they tell her of a map and some hidden information about her mother and father. Then this "father" gives her some cryptic, roundabout message about looking to the "east" and the mother, in a bizarre twist, probably saw him coming down in a parachute... and he might have even *known* her in Shanghai.

Another girl had dreams of events he'd seen in the news... When those two Middle-Easterners, Enoch and some guy who called himself Helias the Tishbite (or was it Elias?), made the news all over the world a few years back with their public messages that drew huge crowds... newspaper editors went nuts. The American media was awkwardly uncomfortable and the men's own two countries' media were seemingly afraid to simply quote what they were saying. They were definitely *not* Muslims. Weird. They were especially ignored after they were kidnapped and ended up in the World Trade Center in New York City when the hijacked airliners ran into the twin towers. Then again, when the press was going crazy reporting everything about terrorists, they couldn't get themselves to mention anything about *these* guys showing up alive again, **on camera** in the streets, after obviously dying way up in the Windows of the World reception room. What they get recorded on their cameras often triggers investigations. At first their own news cameras actually showed them literally floating up with the smoke and ashes, and disappearing into the air several days later... then they censor it, claiming there must be "doctored" or "trick-photography" involved. It seems that ever since then really *crazy* evil stuff has been going on in all the densely populated areas all over the world. The more out of the way, rural areas of the planet seemed much safer.

Several other girls spoke of their dreams... First there was one of that Korean guy who was crowned as the "returning Christ" in a Senate office building... she woke up scared. Then one dreamt of how, just as we did in Japan and Germany after WW-II, the U.S. turned the governments of Afghanistan and Iraq back over to their own people to govern democratically... this happened two days before it was reported in the news. It seemed as though the news never was quite what the media wanted it to be... they just couldn't seem to control the politics of things.

Pebbles of JADE

He'd never had dreams before in his life, but since coming here, he *has* had one about the Middle East... where he has never even been. It was not understandable, but he'd read enough about those two guys the one girl dreamt of to know that something was fundamentally important... or else he was going a little dingy.

And as if all that were not enough to start 'rattling his cage' he now hears about *"visions"* from another girl. This was all beginning to affect him. He needed to get out of here... back to something more normal... back to Yulin on Miyako-Jima.

"Elizabeth, I really cannot help you. I don't know what you saw and all I can do is the same thing you do... speculate. Can we talk about something else? I don't know that I can take much more of this *dream* and *vision* business. I'm getting old. I'm sorry."

"Uhara-san, I'm sorry. You look very tired. Should we start walking back?"

"Yes, I think so. I *am* tired. I probably should head back next week."

"Oh, so soon? You just got here. We really wanted to talk with you more because you remember living there."

"That doesn't make me *psychic*. All of you have trusted me so much and I feel so badly that I can't be of more help... I don't know what all this is about, or what you thought I could do. I've made my plans to leave next week Monday, so I'll be here for another week. Surely I can try to answer all your questions about China by then."

BenOHADI

"Thank you. Thank you. At first I thought I was scaring you away. Should I tell the others about your plans?"

"Yes, I suppose you should. It would be good. It will help keep the discussions to a subject I know something about if they know my time is limited."

Walking next to him she put both arms around his waist and leaned against him as he put an arm around her. "I'm so glad you will be here this week, maybe you would like to come listen as we begin to rehearse for the 'All Saints Day' celebration this Wednesday evening. We always appreciate critiques from non-congregational members because they assist in our 'outreach'. We are especially anxious to introduce you to the rest of our friends in the *full* Church choir."

"I'll be there if you want. Are many of you girls in the choir?"

"We are all in at least one of the choirs. We have three, divided into different age groups. Everyone will be excited to meet you, for the Benjamins and we have spoken of you so often."

I'm a celebrity, Paul thought to himself. This is too much. Peter and Su-mei are locally famous because of what they (especially Su-mei) were able to do in figuring out Chinese Communist Party complicity in the aftermath of the Manhattan terrorist massacre, the attack on the Pentagon and the heroes on the fourth airplane. That informational lead, sent by her while on Miyako, may have *prevented* the implementation of World War III… including disrupting North Korean and Indonesian Islamic plans. Paul felt he should not

Pebbles of JADE

be famous... except maybe *infamous* for almost starting WW-III himself fifty years earlier.

It was getting quite dark by the time they got close to the house and Elizabeth took Paul's hand to keep him from tripping on anything. It felt good to him and brought back memories of his youth. He really did miss those days when he was young and carefree going to school in Hawaii. The one the guys at her school called "the sow" reminded him so much of his own old high school girlfriend so many years ago. He wondered what life would be like after this one. Would heaven just be a life floating on a cloud playing a harp? How would he learn to do that? Who would make the harps? Clouds? What would they be floating over? He was ready for a cup of tea and bed.

Elizabeth said goodnight and went up the stairs when they went in. He went to the kitchen and made some "designer" tea, then went out on the deck to smell and savor the *vanilla-nut* aroma. It was so quiet, peaceful and beautiful out here... and the clean air was refreshing. It truly was an escape from the world's problems... at least for now. He could see why Peter liked it. He thought of Yulin. He was lonely, getting old and wanted a companion in what was left of his life... not only someone to snuggle with, but who honestly enjoyed doing the same things he did with good conversation.

Paul slept well that night. No dreams (or visions), but awoke to the sound of many little feet running up and down the stairway as the girls got ready for school. He waited. When it was quiet and he knew they'd all left, he dressed in a robe and headed for an upstairs shower. After finishing and coming back down, he went past the refectory table in the dining area to get to the kitchen while following the aroma of fresh-brewed coffee. Peter and Su-mei were both sitting on couches in the "great room" holding little girls too young for school and reading the morning paper with their coffee. He joined them.

Everything was quiet for a while. The little ones had eaten and were about to doze back off to sleep. He fixed them each another cup. Soon the girls dropped off and they put them on a small sheet in the middle of the floor, putting light covers over them. There were beads of perspiration on their foreheads. The three adults went onto the deck with their cups and a full pot for some quiet, morning conversation.

"How ya doin', Paul," asked Peter.

"I'm getting old and these young girls are reminding me of it. This place really is pleasant and I can understand why you and Su-mei are here."

"We've wondered if we were 'led' here. Polly tells me you're planning on leaving soon. Is everything okay?"

"Oh yeah. I'm just a little lonely for Yulin and a lot of things have started me thinking since I've been here. Everything is okay. I got some good connections scheduled and the price was too much of an opportunity to pass up. How do you guys do it, Peter? These girls have so much energy!"

"Su-mei does all the work."

"You help," she said.

"That's nice of you Jade, but I know this place and these young ones depend on you. These girls are very blessed to have you." Su-mei had been massaging his neck muscles and bent over and kissed him.

"I'm blessed to have you," she said.

"You guys make me jealous. You think I could get married again?"

"Of course," said Su-mei. "Would you stay on Miyako?"

"Probably. That would be best for both of us. When are you coming out to see us? Old Pete would love to see you again. I guess I'll have to start calling him *Papa* Pete… or maybe *Papa Pirate!"*

They all laughed and Paul continued, "Your friends Maggie and Gail, the singers… remember the *Ladies K.?* Anyway, they said they would play for our reception if we got married in early December when they're back out there again. Think you could come?"

"We'll count our pennies and let you know. For now we want to do some filling in on your life. There's a lot we never had a chance to talk about back in San Fran between the Manhattan massacre and the 'almost war' with Communist China, North Korea and Islamic colonial-like expansionism."

They covered a lot of territory and talked over an hour, until the young ones woke up.

The next week was busy with all the girls' activities, as they continuously were inter-mingling endless conversations with Paul into the night about life in China… often in their pajamas.

Saturday morning exercise and Sunday morning worship came again all too quickly. Time seemed to fly. The worship was just as beautiful as the last time and included a piece they had practiced Wednesday evening.

The title of the sermon in the bulletin read *"A Wonderful Day in Paradise"* and was followed by a printed little picture. Paul assumed the title was talking about the beautiful weather they were having in this wonderful little valley. Noticing the picture was of a theater by that name, he began to doubt his assumption.

For fifteen minutes, while the Sunday School-like transition songs were being sung, people steadily started filling the pews as they came from classrooms. He had found a seat about halfway up the right aisle. The place was soon full, except for the front pews. It became quiet as a violin began softly playing a *prelude*... *"Jesu, Joy of Man's Desiring."* Paul actually found himself praying as the music, coming from behind everyone up in the balcony, caused him to focus his attention on the altar and a large oak carving of Christ suspended directly above it with a crown on his head and outstretched arms in the shape of a cross. It reminded him of the statue of Christ on the mountain in Rio. Memories of his previous life in China with Mari, before she died, came flooding back. She had been responsible for him becoming closer to God in worship... now she was gone and he must responsibly expose Yulin to this contentment of joy he had discovered. But then, he knew she already was a believer. Maybe she was trying to help him?

Pebbles of JADE

The pastor and a woman representing the business administration of the congregation welcomed everyone and had some announcements, and then the service of worship began with hymn number 291, *"Built on the Rock,"* from the large book in the rack behind the pew in front. Wow! Could these people sing! Next, everyone stood to receive the *Trinitarian Invocation*, followed by a public, general confession of sin which allowed for some silent and personal confession, ending with a general absolution by the pastor "in the name of Jesus." The *Introit*, which was King David's Psalm 27, was sung interactively with a soloist in the balcony, who beautifully used a "break" in her voice. Everyone stayed seated while an elder of the congregation read segments from the Old and New Testaments. The pastor then asked everyone to rise in honor of the words of the Christ as he read from the tenth chapter of the Gospel of Saint John, after which everyone sat down again and sang hymn number 515, *"I'm But a Stranger Here."*

The sermon began "When I was a little boy..." Then he held up the picture in the bulletin and continued, "my father would always give me a quarter on Saturday evenings so I could go to the movies with my friends. I would buy my ticket at the window, put it in my pocket and go inside. No one ever collected them. This went on for a long time. Then one night when I was sitting near an 'exit' door and I noticed that just as the lights started to dim and our eyes were adjusting to the dark, someone opened the door so a lot of kids outside could slip in... for free! The following

Saturday night I thought about that. If I stood outside that door, I could get in free too... and save my quarter. As I felt the quarter in my pocket given me for free by my father, I dismissed the thought, bought my ticket and went inside the way I'd been taught. As it happened, *that night*, after the lights dimmed... they came back up again without the movie starting. A man came down the aisle followed by two ushers with flashlights. He announced there would be a ticket check... would everyone please hold up their tickets for the ushers to check. After I'd reached in my pocket and produced mine, I noticed about a dozen young people being escorted from the theater... the Hollywood landmark *Paradise Theater*. It felt so good to not be judged "guilty" and subsequently driven out of the *Paradise* because I was prepared with the ticket that was a free gift from a loving father. The story is true. The moral is obvious. Now let me tell you of the *true* Paradise... the eternal and almighty Father of everything who loves us, the *Good News* of the free gift of His eternal and perfect Son sacrificed to suffer, bleed and die, in substitution for each and all of us.

"The history is true. Now the *rest* of the story... Do not use your God-given, independent human willpower to call the testimony of the Holy Spirit a lie, thereby rejecting what has already been paid-in-full *for* you by the Grace of God."

The sermon included a lot more, reflecting on historically recorded Roman culture during Jesus' day and the ungodly influences upon the Hebrew tribal cultures of Abraham's day. Paul thought to himself,

"Thank God for the faith of that very young Hebrew girl named Mary. Because of her faith and belief in God and His messenger, Gabriel (a *he,* or a *she*?), she was the most blessed of all women in human history… having borne the human body that animated the eternal Tao, Mary's own Savior also." All Paul could think of was how blessed he and his Mari were… and now he must explain all this to Yulin and old Pete. Or did they know and understand? Would there be an historic house of Christian worship and prayer on Miyako-Jima? Pirate Pete and Yulin were Christians of some kind… they would know.

Standing, they publicly recited the Nicene Creed together and the pastor prayed a bunch of prayers that had been passed to him by the ushers from the collection plates… and everyone concluded with the Lord's Prayer. He then blessed the congregation with a *Benediction* and walked to the back of the *Nave*, everyone sat, sang number 404 *"Take My Life…"* and he dismissed them to "Go in peace… serve the Lord."

The *Faithful* were then invited to remain for the *Eucharist,* which he assumed would last another ten minutes or so. Earlier he had been told he would always be welcome to receive instruction so he could be in communion with them… which all were invited to confessionally do.

As many made their way back to the parish fellowship hall, Paul asked if they ever changed the 'service' as he looked around at some of the *Polly Brigade* sitting near him who had not yet completed their catechism instruction. The response made him feel a little stupid.

Sharp, petite Anna spoke up and explained, "It is *always* changing! We have different opening songs, 'readings', hymns, prayers, sermons and choral pieces each time."

"No, I mean the 'liturgy'... does *it* ever change?"

"It changes a little throughout the Church Year, but only because we practice it every Sunday can we make it sound so good. We keep polishing it... to make it the best of our vocal art we can offer. Why would we want to change it? The *Liturgy* is what ties all the things that *change* together every Sunday."

Polly added, "We found it actually attracts people because, we think, people are tiring of how lazy and overly casual Americans have become in the last century. At least that's what we think we are figuring out. An appreciation of the deeper-thinking style of an earlier culture is possibly beginning a resurgence, a renaissance, just as in the Middle Kingdom of China... while correcting for mistakes made, especially in the respect for human life and the authority of God's Word. Elona Li and her parents think people, especially the young boys, are just attracted to all the girls. They were just joking, I think."

The depth of thinking evident in the *Polly Brigade* never ceased to amaze Paul. Even if they were practicing Christians, he still was going to have a lot to share with Yulin and old Pete. His flight would leave tomorrow, so packing had to begin this afternoon... and a point was made in his mind to talk a little with each of

Pebbles of JADE

the girls today while saying goodbye. He was really going to miss them and could never forget them... they had changed his life!

After many more introductions and visits, the two vans finally headed back out to *Brigadoon* at the Depot. While those on duty began preparing for lunch on the deck, Su-mei was helping him wash clothes and pack when she stopped what she was doing and looked directly into Paul's eyes.

"Paul, I have a confession."

"Uh, oh."

"No," she continued with her trademark, deep giggle. "It's nothing bad. But after what the girls have told me, I was afraid to mention that I, too, had a dream...

"Now don't get excited! I'm not going to ask you to explain it. It was just a pleasantly curious thing... and many others that we associate with around here have also mentioned having dreams. Personally, I think something is about to happen... not necessarily *bad*, mind you, just important."

"Well, here I go again. It appears my purpose in coming here was to bring out all of the 'dreams'... Ok, sorry, what was yours about?"

"I'm sorry too, but I won't ask you to interpret anything... I only thought you should at least know about it. It started with a vision of Peter standing behind me as we soaked in the view from a beautiful little terrace in front of a landmark called the 'Jade Screen Tower' while he encouraged me to look out across the expanse of the mountains and misty valleys.

BenOHADI

He told me the whole earth again belonged to all of us for our enjoyment… compliments of God's methodical grace when He had rescued the last of humans He foresaw as *faithful* and chose the exact, split-second moment to reveal it. That was it. I woke up. That was the night before you arrived."

"Really? That's it? How did it make you feel?"

"Deliriously happy… but I don't know why. I was full of a very deep joy when I woke."

"Well, that's good. That's the shortest one so far, including my own. Where *is* this place you described. Did you recognize it?"

She looked at him with a twinkle in her eyes. "Oh, you had one too, did you?" She laughed and continued, "My parents told me they went there for their honeymoon. They loved it. I've never been there, but it is high up in Huangshan Mountain. They said you could see the *whole world* from up there. Maybe someday Peter and I will visit the place… maybe he had the same dream. It is not too far from the Jade House they now call *Shangri-la*. Surely the new dam will not cause the river to rise *that* high… if it's ever finished," she laughed again and went back to the washing.

* * *

He felt closer than he had ever been to Peter and Su-mei and it was hard to leave, but soon he must depart this little *paradise*.

Pebbles of JADE

His *moment* of departure early the next morning took almost an hour with the continuous hugging and crying and all the little ones who kept thinking up something more they just *had* to tell him. How could they be so awake at five in the morning? He was becoming emotionally drained! He felt badly about having to leave so early, but the flight that made a good connection through Portland left Boise at nine. He would have liked to seen San Fran again, but what was left of it was still in a very messy reconstruction phase after those giant tidal waves some years back. Finally, he just stepped backward out the door, got into his car and made one last announcement from the rolled-down window as they all came out the front door under the porch-light and out onto the circular driveway around the old stone outdoor fireplace…

"All of you… come see me sometime! I'm going to miss all of you so much! Pray for me… for *us!*" Then he waved, blew them a kiss and kind-of *gunned* away regretfully… allowing himself to sob out-loud, softly and with a smile, until he reached the highway going south… something he would never do in front of people. Getting out his handkerchief to wipe his eyes and clean his glasses, he noticed what a clear night it was. The black sky over East Mountain was slowly showing some blue as the faithful and inevitable sun seemed to be pushing the bright stars to the west.

The drive down the winding mountain highway took close to two hours because of his unfamiliarity with the road and the distracting, beautiful moonlit landscape through the river and tree-lined canyons…

eventually the sunrise took over as it cast its dark shadows in the canyons. He kept slowing down to soak up the view. The place was naturally beautiful... maybe he should bring Yulin up here into the Mountain West sometime. She's never seen what so much of America used to look like. She only sees the pictures of disaster areas on TV.

Yulin. The almost three weeks he'd spent with Peter, Su-mei and all those girls made him realize how much he needed Yulin. He yearned for the touch of her hand, the press of her skin... anywhere, everywhere, almost always! Without her, as it had been with Mari, he felt he was only *half there!* He had so much to tell her... where to begin? And... what about old Pirate Pete? Neither he, nor his flying buddy and future father-in-law, had that many years left and he cared a lot for him too. He resolved to start praying for them both regularly. Thank God they both were at least Christians... it would make things a lot easier. In fact, thinking back on some things they'd said... they might have had a stronger faith than he did in those early days of their acquaintance. He had always been the spiritually weak one! "Be sure to give them a call from Portland between flights to let them know he was on his way and how the scheduled time was working out," he reminded himself.

It took him almost three hours to get down the mountain, across town to the airport, get the rental car checked in, and then get himself checked in at the ticket counter so he could check his bag. It took another forty-five minutes to get through security and out to the gate... but he made it... and was en-route to Portland, then to Tokyo, from where he would catch a smaller plane to Miyako-Jima. He had a lot to think about all the way to what was probably going to be his last home.

* * *

The leg to Portland was uneventful. Good thing he had a bagel and cream cheese with some coffee during the few minutes he was early at the gate, because juice and another cup of coffee was the extent of the service once airborne.

Upon arrival he did remember to make his phone call and was encouraged to hear Yulin's voice. Her father was anxious to see him again also, she said, because he didn't think he was going to live much longer and had something important to tell him... she didn't know what. "Well," responded Paul. "I have something important to tell you both also. I also have something to ask you..." and the phone went dead. When he tried to call back, all he got was a recorded message saying there was difficulty on the line. Oh, well. It wouldn't be too much longer and he would be there... and they now had his schedule.

* * *

On the ten-hour leg to Japan he kept dreaming every time he dozed off to sleep. It got to where he found himself deliberately trying to go back to sleep whenever he could, because he had never experienced much dreaming and now the visions in these dreams started tying together and making more sense. Was he actually thinking better in his sleep? He was getting a little excited about getting back to sleep... which didn't help any.

Ling Sao Jade had given him her favorite book of poetry, with frayed pages, to read on the way home. She told him it was one of her prize possessions... so would he please take care of it? It surprised him to find out it was *not* the writings of any famous Chinese poets.

He just finished eating the in-flight dinner they served and was enjoying an expensive seven-dollar glass of *B&B*, his favorite liquor, while he finished reading the little book. The experience of the emotionally charged, ever changing rhythms of John Milton's *"Paradise Lost"* was moving. His mind immediately went back to Mel Gibson's *"Passion of the Christ"* movie that came out some years past... and how the two works stood in such contrast as each epitomized to the media of their generation. In Milton's day people read books. Who would have expected Gibson, the handsome movie star, to become the first in this new millennium to be thought of as a *hero of the Faith*? Together, both of them seemed to make recorded history so clearly understandable. Both used their artistic talented skill in altruistic ways.

Closing his eyes, he slowly came to realize he really did believe in this God Milton and Gibson had portrayed... and in His strong, eternal proclamation, the *Word* finally born into human flesh who promised to rescue him, Paul, and all believers. Awesome!

Pebbles of JADE

Looking at his watch he realized it was just midnight according to his biological clock. He drifted into another very dreamy sleep while listening to Norah Jones singing "Come Away With Me" coming so romantically through his headset... then it seemed to transition into an old version of "At Last." How God must love his human creation! He felt, to use a word Su-mei had recently used, *deliriously* happy.

As his head leaned against the little window, he noticed it very dark and moonless out... except for the meteor shower that attracted his attention. The sky was full of streaks of light... he had never seen so many "shooting stars"! Then the sky was suddenly black. Yet, there was no cloud cover or bad weather around. Suddenly he was wide-awake to a sharp, clear sound. Was that a trumpet he heard? Some kind of aircraft warning signal? He'd never heard anything like that! It was so loud and absolutely pure sounding!

He no longer had his headset on, yet he heard so many beautiful voices singing together so powerfully... this wasn't making sense. Was he dreaming of some really old movie, like "2001, A Space Odyssey" or the sequel "2010" something?

Suddenly there was *earth* under his feet and he saw all the *Polly Brigade* girls! His mind seemed to be whirling. There was Peter, Su-mei and all of their families including Peter's first wife Lei, who looked like Su-mei's twin, and their children... even some of his old friends he had flown with in the Strategic Air Command when their B-47 had gone down in China... "My God," he thought to himself. "Those are my

BenOHADI

parents over there... and my friends from China... and my wonderful Mari! This is not making any sense... it's **impossible**! No one is noticing me... but then, how could they in this enormous sea of people? There must be millions of them out there! Do they even see me? Oh, that's the problem with dreams," he chuckled to himself... then he again realized he was standing on *terra firma,* not reclining in an airline seat!

* * *

He wasn't in an airplane... and no matter how hard he tried, he *couldn't* wake up. Touching and feeling his body made him realize he was already very awake and he could clearly understand there were no drugs involved... he was thinking clearly. This was no dream, but how did he get here... and where did all these people come from? Where was he? Everyone appeared to be focusing their attention on that hill over there with those huge white things on top... Are those thrones? There are people way up there where everything is so bright... as brilliant as the sun, yet everyone was easily looking at it... miles and miles of people! Curiously, he seemed to recognize everyone, even when so far away. This is surreal! Just then he heard brass and string instruments and everyone was singing. He heard things! He couldn't remember ever *hearing* anything in a dream before... and all the colors were so vivid and *smelled* so good! Everything was so tangible...this was *not* a dream!

Pebbles of JADE

His name was called... and looking around he recognized the face of Lili Jade Green, just as bright as ever...but different, much more mature looking. She was grabbing his hand and pulled him to her, hugging him. Then he realized something that curiously did not bother him a bit. His parents up ahead of him, none of the *Jade* family, not even himself were wearing anything! Yet he felt everyone was clothed... there was no sense of embarrassment, much less any *shame*. Then he saw Yulin and old Pete, but they didn't look old anymore and were *so* excited to see him. In a moment, his mother was standing next to him, but she looked liked pictures he remembered in his clear, but rapidly fading memory, of when she was a young woman.

"It is *so* good to see you again!" she exclaimed.

"You, too, Mama," he answered. "It was so long ago, and you look wonderful!"

"Oh, no dear. It was just a moment ago when you were standing by my bed and I told you about the angels I heard singing again... just as I had many years ago that time I was so afraid. I saw the brightness of that throne up there and suddenly here we are! Isn't this wonderful? Oh, I must see Him... and then so many others..." and she vanished.

There was a giant family reunion going on all around him with folks recognizing each other across the time-lines of all the human generations. Looking at his hands, he realized he didn't feel or look old anymore either. He was "recognizing" people from history he knew he could not have ever met. How did he do that?

What was going on? What kind of dream... but he *knew* he was not dreaming! Lili squeezed his hand and he heard her say, "We **will** always thank Him." Paul knew that even before she pointed to the radiant person sitting on the top of the hill with a crown of, what looked light, pure light on his head. She continued enthusiastically, "He made you a simple believer in the Messiah of God, Jesus of Nazareth... Then His power in you enabled you to trust Him so he could rescue you from the chaotic meltdown, purging with fire, and reforming that His Spirit has just very quickly caused to happen. His **"Day"** finally came! This is the *One* we were taught to look for in the *Jade Homes*. In His Son we see the Father of everything... who *loves* us!" This was not new in Paul's mind, but was quickly clarified. All that was in him wanted to always praise God for doing the humanly impossible! Mankind had always dreamt of a *utopia*... but it was impossible to achieve. However, not for God!

Lili and he noticed powerful looking *beings* who seemed to be in charge of things were wearing beautiful clothes... yet also seemed to have the same *thick air* around them.

Lili squealed, "One of them just told me all the 'human-stuff' had just been *redone* for us...whatever that means. So much seems to be happening almost instantly! All the singing we hear is everyone's response to the awesome power of *Him*... that was hidden from us when He came as a human... back when there was 'time' that we lived in. He proved who

He was, but so many didn't want to 'see' it. Denial of reality. It wasn't how they wanted things to be."

Paul knew he was definitely not asleep anymore. In fact, it felt he was just finally waking up from a bad... and really dangerous dream he could barely remember. He wasn't even interested in exactly what might have happened. He was interested to know he was totally safe, had never felt this *excited* ever before in his life, and it seemed this was what he had always subconsciously yearned for. Now it was here, so suddenly, when he was least expecting it.

A memory from the beginning of human time came into his mind. He had not been there... how could he be remembering it? But, there it was... like a vision. He saw the planet earth, as if from above, with an enormous number of angels being banished to it... except for one gorgeous spot. In it there was one human... then it was divided into two people, male and female, and told to "multiply and *subdue* the earth and everything in it." They were able to communicate with all of the other life-forms, especially with the animals, within the limits of their minds regarding cooperative interaction.

The archangel in control of the other angels who rebelled with him found it desirable to roam the new physical creation, especially *earth* with its air-breathing creatures. He soon figured out *his* spirit could live inside the animals, so he chose one that already had the capability to ask the humans some questions... so they would not be surprised. In that way he slipped into the special grounds made just for humans and talked to them through their minds. He found them particularly naïve... they had no experiential education and were easily tricked out of what God had given them. The archangel, Lucifer, now had ownership of the beautiful human area also, with its special trees. One of the trees provided fruit that would provide all the nutrition they would ever need to fuel their bodies forever and its leaves could provide all the medication they would ever need. The other tree was *brain food* and would have slowly provided all the intellectual growth they needed as fast as God determined they could be brought up to speed regarding the *image of God*. Ultimately they would grow and multiply so as to take control of the whole planet... outnumber, and once fully developed in the image of God, leave no place for the soon-to-be banished angels to hide.

The unfaithful archangel was quick, grabbed an opportunity when these new humans might easily submit to temptation and his gamble paid off... they were not faithful to God. Lucifer and his spirit tribe were excited. The four-dimensional physical realm of this new world had not been made for them. It was sort of an ocean around the "pit" they'd been exiled to... and the "pit" of the earth was *awful* isolation. They *might* be able to spiritually live inside and subtly control a variety of these human animals that *could* reproduce and become powerful slaves, while at the same time *they* could experience the humans' physical world... which would be a great life for them! The size of the archangel's tribe was too small and he needed more numbers. However, like the mortal animals, some of the humans would be overwhelmed and not of much use. However, if they *could* possess these humans kept alive by their special fruit and merely educate them to *his* evil mission, he might *still* be able to overthrow YHWH, prove how smart and powerful he was... and take control of everything, forever! The vision ended as abruptly as it began. Paul shook his head.

A Voice, not particularly loud but heard by everyone as one of absolute authority, started speaking and everyone became silent. Just as strongly as he felt himself and those around him being magnetically drawn to the Voice, he saw so many millions more being repelled away from the great white throne and powerfully being sucked into a vortex. In the blackness of it he saw the faces of Lucifer and the angels he'd seen in the vision. The center of the hole was a sort of extremely hot, black-fire nothingness and those being drawn to it had a look of horror on their faces.

Looking for anyone identifiable, he could see many to whom great intelligence might have been given, others appeared to have great physical stature, still others looked quite young, many were very little children... even innocent looking babies... but they too were stained and spiritually sick looking. All were so sapped of any fighting spirit, so weak looking and *all* lacked energy or any kind of strength, were unrecognizable... and, surprisingly, he didn't even *want* to know or have anything to do with them, even if he had been able to identify them. There was no compassion, just repulsion. He felt different. Was he being protected?

Resistance to the pull exerted on them by the black hot vortex was recognizably impossible, hopeless. Paul knew *they* now knew they would consciously exist in their terribly weak bodies eternally... and not be able to die. They had not lost their new immortality, just any possibility of *glory*! Who and how many had failed them during life on earth in their once mortal bodies? Somehow he knew they had just been shown their lives and sinful inner-being in some sort of 'trial' he and the others would *not* experience. He felt so terribly sorry for them, but there was nothing anyone was able... or even wanted to do. Everyone wanted all evil to be gone forever. It seemed some law of physics was kicking in. In a flash it was over, the painful memory of it rapidly faded... and a wonderful sense of Milton's "lusciousness" came over him as he heard an enormous choir of angels singing. **Home** *at last*!

* * *

As what looked for a moment to be millions and millions of people were being herded away by powerful looking beings (angels?), there appeared behind them, in front of the King's throne, an ever expanding banquet table with everything imaginable spread out on it as a feast. The King Himself was standing at the head of it. Something inside him explained he was observing beings known as Seraphim above the throne and Cherubim surrounded it. They were all singing.

Paul realized he was recognizing people he never met, or even saw real pictures of, sitting up near the

Pebbles of JADE

King... There was Mary of Nazareth, Paul of Tarsus, Peter of Galilee and all the original apostles, plus the famous David, Jacob, Abraham, Elisha and Elijah, Moses, Noah, Jonah, even Abel, Eve and Adam... and many, many earliest Church Fathers. Behind them all were thousands upon thousands of those who died trusting in the true YHWH alone and the eternal Proclamation who would arrive in human flesh.

Then there was the King himself. Mother Mary's little *Lamb* was indeed as white as bright snow... but now had the demeanor of a powerful and satisfied Lion. Gazing in awe at the spectacle, his eyes swept over that group near the front. Apostle Paul had the aggressive look of a young scholar in a university, but with tears in his eyes as he worshipped his Savior. And Apostle Peter... he was a much larger young man than expected... and had a full, black beard. So this was the little "pebble" Jesus had spoken to when he proclaimed how blessed he was to have received from the Holy Spirit the boulder-like *Faith* in the eternal Son of God... finally here on earth in the flesh of his beloved mankind.

Paul was mesmerized. His old friend, Peter, and Su-mei came up and joined Lili and him as they all knelt in the grass. Su-mei uttered in that deep voice that used to give him jealous shivers, "Can you believe we have all been in the traditional succession of the *Faith* from Adam to Abraham to David to Mary and the Apostle Peter... and to us?"

Lili hugged her *Grandmother* and sobbed, "And we've all been your little *pebbles*...Thank you! Thank you Father. Thank you, King Jesus, for being the *Rock* that always followed us all throughout history!"

Soon the King held up in welcome a huge, sparkling, beautiful crystalline glass of wine... and asked everyone to join him. Paul could feel a taste of wine on his palette. It was really there...and he swallowed.

The King said, **"The table will always be here... you are always welcome and invited to join in and indulge yourselves *in me* and all I have for you. We have much to talk about... forever and ever."**

The King was recognizably a human... and Paul knew it was *Jesus*, God's historically promised Messiah he'd heard so much about and learned to trust. This was the beginning of a new *learning* process, but he sensed some *un*-learning was also part of it... some vocabulary recognized for a moment... was vanishing. He heard the King gently explain to everyone (yet everyone could hear him) "From before you knew me, I have always been. I became one of you and lived with you as a son of Adam. You became part of me. I repented *for* you, I suffered *for* you, I bled *for* you and I died *for* you. I came back to life as a human to show you what I would do *for* you... and I still am and always will be with you as your human brother. The Father of everything loves you and the creative power of the Spirit will always empower you.

"As humans, we are all children of Adam. We have all been cut from the same generation of human cloth. Before anything was created, however, the Father and I are eternally *one*... which means you are one with God

Pebbles of JADE

and all Creation through me. For God is everything that exists... which is why God is everywhere, totally powerful and has even created all knowledge. I am the eternal Father's "Voice" and the "Spirit" is his creative hand since the beginning of everything. YHWH is eternal intelligence. And since I am part of *them*, you can always communicate through me, your brother, to YHWH because I am also part of you. You originally knew us as YHWH, but piously referred to us as the LORD... yet I told you I AM the Alpha and the Omega, the beginning and the end of all life, physical matter and energy as you know it.

"The original unity we had was twisted into disunity by the Evil one. Now everything, beginning with you, has been reborn into its originally designed form. Because all evil has been swept away, all of your contaminated nature is swept away also. Remember the *washing* and the *burning*? Look around you while I will repeat myself from the time I was with you before, but this time you will understand...

"Hear me, all of you, and understand: There is nothing outside a person that by going into him can defile him, the things that come out of a person are what defile him. Do you not see that whatever goes into a person from outside cannot defile him, since it enters not his heart but his stomach, and is expelled? What comes out of a person is what defiles him. For from within, out of the heart of man, come evil thoughts, sexual immorality, theft, murder, adultery, coveting, wickedness, deceit, sensuality, envy, slander, pride, foolishness. All these evil things come from within, and they defile a person."

He looked around and waved everyone to be seated. The benches, low stone walls and grassy slopes were wonderfully comfortable and convenient. Then he continued...

"All those who lived in the latter days heard those words through my student Mark. The influence of Lucifer and his followers (you knew him as Satan and the demons) has been removed. Those humans who rejected me until the end of their *time*, deliberately or ignorantly while under the evil rebellious influence of Satan's world, have also been removed. Many were lost when so many of you proudly shirked your responsibility to deliver my grace in baptism, much less share my *body and blood* to help them grow stronger. You asked in my name and, by the Father's grace, were forgiven for all your sin, including your own *deliberate* ignorance regarding my *total* presence in your midst, which could have helped you help others. You, but not those you deprived of my baptismal "cloak of righteousness" before they could learn to understand your earthly tongue and died, were forgiven. Many of you denied my grace even to your babies... and now, you alone who finally, but *intellectually*, accepted my grace by obediently becoming *one* with me in baptism, will I continue to always be with. Why did you arrogantly insist on trusting your own rational minds more than my grace? While I was with you before, my students spent three years learning to understand my teaching to their ancestors. Many years later you only paid *selective* attention to what they passed on... because you corrupted the word "tradition." You can only imagine the enormity of the guilt I have lifted from you in my Father's forgiveness... and in my mercy, you will forget how you failed the responsibility I gave you to care for others with *sacramentum* given you by the true, gracious, loving God.

"Now, most of what you learned while in the *womb of the old world of sin* must also be taken away from your minds because it is contaminated and you will never again be tormented with it. Your days of suffering and tribulation are finally over. It was worse for you than Lucifer allowed you to think it was on his earth... which your original parents, Adam and Eve, in my beautiful garden actually *gave* him and thwarted my first plan."

Then the King... the incarnate Word we knew as Yeshua, Jesu, or Jesus... wept.

As he finished speaking, there was a powerful *rushing* sound. Paul sensed the memory of what was just said, along with a great amount of useless *worldly* knowledge and vocabulary being sucked from him and everyone else as small tongues of fire appeared momentarily on their heads. Then in a swirl of gray and black with the accompanying smell of death, the phenomena vanished as a howling wind following those who had been ushered out a moment before. The wind and black fire became silent in a dark, closing hole that sealed and vanished into the bright sky. The black dot vanished... never to be seen or remembered again.

They all looked around at what surrounded them... a huge, beautiful, bright, seemingly flawless city made of clear and translucent stones of different shades, flowing with soft, luminous gold-colored roads leading everywhere... everything entwined with gardens, birds and small animals. There were shops, clothing stores and restaurants... even office buildings.

People had started *milling around* everywhere... exploring, it seemed. Time was slowing down again. Everyone from every race and generation were able to talk with each other, *understandably*, trying to figure out what to do... since they'd come to realize they would always want to worship God *while* doing whatever else they wanted at the same time. Some went back and forth to the banquet table, talked with the King (how did he do that?) and visited. They all seemed to have different ideas and were able to put them to work without any difficulty... just had to figure it out, and had eternity to accomplish everything. In the restaurant the four of them stepped into, they were told by the helpers to choose or ask for anything desired. The variety of specialty business allowed for Peter, his Jade, Lili, Paul and everyone to find satisfaction. The "helpers" actually identified themselves as *angels* whose duty it was to temporarily be humans and help everyone get started, then continue to help when asked or needed... as people adjusted to working with spirits, their only natural form.

Pebbles of JADE

A haunting memory flashed back in his mind... there was no money, nor any need for any. But, what *was* money? They could just *have* whatever they wanted. It was not until they were in a clothing store he realized he would always be able to *have* whatever he wanted, so there was no need to be greedy. Again he curiously wondered, "What did *'greedy'* mean... he seemed to have forgotten, and was not interested in trying to remember as he tried on a few items. Was he now a child, learning again... in a fully-grown body? There were also children's stores, music stores, markets and schools. The sounds and smells and colors were gentle, yet much more extreme from subtle to vivid... and *so* pleasurable. Plants and flowers gave off sweet aromas and were everywhere. So were the rainbow plumage of birds and so many other animals... including the fish in the streams! Animals were only where people wanted them to be... they seemed to know, but because there were so many that were so different than seen before, there was much curiosity... and there was no fear!

He also noticed that while different people had different tastes, it did not make much difference, everyone seemed to genuinely care for each other and there was no reason to be judgmental, jealous or feel any need for control over other people... everyone knew there was nothing to gain! Again, some of those thoughts and words did not seem to make any sense any more. Something very strange was happening to him. Something about him seemed to have (thank God) vanished... and associated thoughts were fading, a total adjustment of heart and mind, without any regret. There was so much more to learn!

It finally dawned on him that when so many were being sort-of *herded* away (did he really remember that happening?), something also changed in the atmosphere. Everything smelled new, fresh and fragrant. Everything seemed so *alive*! Several of them were enjoying a variety of coffees, teas and other drinks of all kinds while talking this new experience over… all their senses seemed greatly expanded. Everyone seemed to easily understand and control their indulgence in everything lest it strain their body.

What were they supposed to do? Where were they? How big was this world they were on? Was there anything besides this gorgeous city? Was there industry, agriculture or even countryside? They all started hearing all sorts of things in their heads and they knew they were in touch with a magnificent God who was answering their questions through His powerful, creative Spirit. They were on a new "earth" the same size as the old one before the purifying, with rivers and canyons, mountains and woods, lakes, oceans and beaches… even deserts. Everything was there (again?). Except… no sin-infection, human death, or even pain and suffering of any kind. Also, there were no borders in the Kingdom of God… and the way humans and nature were designed to interact, formerly known as "the Law", was written on everyone's heart. It had always been there, but now people paid attention to that *"still, small Voice."* Paul wondered if he could just look around by himself a little…

Pebbles of JADE

In a flash, he was alone. What happened to the others? It seemed he was now part of the air itself. He was wherever he wanted to be, exploring. Did he have control of the molecules of his body as it interacted with all the other molecules in the universe? Sometimes he was looking at the landscape... rural countryside with both wild and domestic animals... some he did not recognize as having seen before, and he sensed a degree of communication with them. There was also both wild, undeveloped *and* cultivated land. Other times he was in buildings and homes... exploring. Nothing seemed hidden.

Once he wanted to ask a guy who was standing a long way away a question about something... and in the blink of an eye he found himself standing next to him to do so. The person did not seem alarmed, just had a little surprised smile. Suddenly, as he asked him, he realized he already knew the man's name and could easily communicate with him... and that the man came from an era on earth many thousands of years before his own. The fleeting memory vanished. They both had many questions to ask, as if they were small children learning all sorts of new things from each other, having just met each other on a playground. The tour with the guy of his nearby home was amazing. It was a very primitive little thatched hut that was clean, quite comfortable and actually very colorfully beautiful in its naturalness. It had everything the man wanted for the moment, but he was busy learning all sorts of new things, especially in what Paul used to call "technology"... even though that word didn't seem to fit well anymore because so much more could be done without any electronic machinery. The man was educated differently, but very smart. Everyone seemed smart... everyone had a direct connection with the ultimate intelligence of the universe and beyond! Looking around, he concluded there were many relatives and other like-minded people living nearby for this man, because he saw many other similar dwellings in a village-like setting. Paul wondered where he himself would live... he knew it would be a totally satisfying pleasure, but did not want to think about that just yet... because he knew what would happen if he did. It excited him to realize he had a certain control over his body's interaction with the universe around him!

For a moment Lili was next to him again and said, "You're hard to keep up with. I'll join up again later"... and she was gone.

When he was finished and wanted to move on, he found himself "in" the air again. This was going to take a little getting used to... sort of like how it must have been when learning how to walk. He *must* learn to control his thoughts carefully. That was when he noticed *vehicles* on a road. The people in them were visiting. Could he do that? Suddenly, there he was, sitting with some of them in the one he'd been looking at. They laughed and said, "Welcome aboard. Don't worry, if it gets crowded someone will leave. It's happened before," and they all laughed again. One of them explained to him it was taking them *all* a little time to figure out how to live in this new world, but they all knew it was going to be much better than they could imagine so far. They were now *both* spiritual *and* human beings! Even their imaginations were growing. They each were telling the others what they had been discovering regarding resources, materials, commodities and services... even *seminars* some called *councils*. Everything seemed well established and they were all welcome to jump in wherever they felt best qualified, knowledgeable, or even just interested. Supplies of everything were inexhaustible and no money (?) or credit (?) was needed. He tried to remember the meaning of a word: "worry"(?). Yet, it made no sense to him. He knew he had changed.

When he asked how long they had been here, they all answered they did not know. It seemed they had just been born and only had occasional flashbacks... each from different places and different historical eras. That was a little confusing, but they all were having their *flashes* less and less often. No one could really remember much about what was before... even though they all seemed to recognize, but did not exactly *know* each other... that would take a little time. A couple mentioned it was as if they had just been delivered from a womb... except they understood that to have been a solo experience *usually*. One thing they all did know was this was the most non-selfish, pleasurable, exciting, adventurous life they could imagine and they felt so "connected" with everything, especially God... whom they could not help but always praise! God was everywhere and glorious! They were now out of the *shadow-lands* and everyone seemed to be able to *see*...

understand what they were learning. Previous life for everyone now seems to have only been a *shadow* of what was to come. Yet, no one seemed concerned about the future... because they knew it was endless. There always was plenty of everything... and unlimited time. In fact, the word "time" now seemed a little confusing. Clocks and watches were only used to schedule activities, not keep any track of ages of things or people.

"Where can we go?"

"Anywhere."

"How? Are there other forms of transportation, like airplanes?"

"Yes, but they are not necessary. They just provide the ability for us to *visit* and discuss plans while traveling. Or, they are for the fun of it. By yourself you can just materialize wherever you want. If you get hurt, no problem... the body heals itself and is rejuvenated by fruit and leaves from a special tree that grows everywhere."

"How do you know all this?"

"We asked God. He immediately comes to our mind with limitless, encyclopedic (?) information to help us learn whatever we want as we endlessly learn more."

"Is there *space* travel? I think I was always interested in what is out there."

"Yes of course. It will be up to you to figure out *why* you are interested and what you want to do with what you find... everything was made intelligently with a purpose. Space is infinite, so you can just explore all you want. Just remember, if you materialize in your

Pebbles of JADE

body so you can study and feel things sensually, your body will have to breathe air, cope with pressure changes and different gravitational forces and eat... so you have to plan ahead. If you find the necessary resources you can develop whatever you want, wherever. God will give you all the information you seek."

"Does that special tree grow everywhere? Even on lifeless planets?"

No one had ever asked that question, so they all just shrugged their shoulders and giggled. One small, very young and dark-skinned person with bright, hazel eyes spoke up in a high voice... "Fruit and leaves are *portable*, so just take some along with you everywhere." Suddenly, with a shake of the head she continued... "Some stuff once called 'manna' had everything humans needed, besides water, to survive for forty years. The birds were flown in to provide for the greed of the other senses." That made sense, as he realized everyone here was not yet fully-grown in stature... yet, *no* one looked old.

Suddenly Ling Sao appeared and Paul exclaimed, "Ling Sao Jade Fragrant! Oh, it is so good to see you! I've seen a lot of people I knew, but you're the first one I can visit with... must be one of those fleeting memories." They just stood and hugged for a while. "You are more beautiful than ever... I think. This new life is truly a dream come true... but still a little confusing."

"Well, of one thing I'm not confused... you're pretty dashing and handsome yourself, young man. I won't call you *beautiful*, even though you are, because I don't think you are used to that yet."

Everyone else in the vehicle laughed as they realized they could still blush.

For a few moments, Elona Li appeared dressed in a beautiful, green silk-brocade, oriental dress. All she said was, "Welcome. I'm making the rounds to see everyone I once knew before. Enjoy your reunion. I am en-route to a council meeting called by our legion's archangel. Please understand, we are all equal, but have different characteristics and attributes. We no longer fight against evil, so our mission has changed. I will visit with you to explain many things later." Then she was gone. She looked more powerful and a little different. *She?*

After a little silence while they all just studied each other, they discussed how they all knew their physical appearance must be different than it was before. One person spoke up and said God told him we used to be divided as male and female as most plants and animals still were, but now every human was a whole person, physical *and* spiritual, entire unto themselves.

Paul noticed *the Sao* was in a sort of trance with a happy, but far-away look in her eyes... she was trembling and there was a little perspiration on her brow, so he asked, "Are you alright? Would you like to get away and do some exploring together for a little while?"

"Oh, I'm definitely alright... and yes, I'd like that," Ling Sao smiled with an unsteady, but bubbling and confident voice.

Paul looked at her quizzically, "Do you know where your home is? I haven't thought or asked about mine yet... but I want to. I will soon. I'm just trying to discipline my thoughts. Maybe you would like to join me so we can just walk and talk a little?" Paul explained how he thought he should be overwhelmed, but he wasn't. He heard sounds he had never imagined and saw and smelled so much more in a surprising way. All his *senses* seemed so dramatically powerful.

"No I don't know where I'll call home. But yes, I would like to know. Will you check it out with me? We can get out and walk right over there, I think," she laughed. "I'm like you, I also think I should be overwhelmed and I'm trying hard to control how I interact in this new environment... and how did I know where to get off? Want to go?"

"Sure," and *bang*, they both knew where to go and what to look for.

The Sao laughed, bubbling, "Let's do this the old-fashioned way... and *walk*. I need it... the pleasure of using my body."

There were puffy clouds in a brilliantly blue sky, beautiful clear air and the sun was shining brightly, but they noticed as they walked away from the banquet table in what seemed to be the center of the new city, the surrounding light became less intense. There were gentle shadows caused by the sun, but it wasn't needed... there was no true *darkness* anywhere... or was it their eyes seemed to be so much better? They could see, and even hear anything they looked at... even fairly long distances if they wanted to.

BenOHADI

"I'll race you," shouted Paul as they both started running to the outskirts of the new city... which they'd learned was called "Peace." The luminous, gold road was soft and comfortable to run on and they were soon out in the beautiful, manicured countryside... running and running across lush grass now and not getting tired. They didn't even think about out-running, or *beating* the other. It was fun to stretch out their leaps before touching down and bounding off again... almost like flying. Finally they stopped, panted a little and looked at each other in amazement. They had run for what must have been many miles, had passed towns and villages, and were now standing outside a quaint little cluster of small homes that had natural wood framed sliding doors with papered grids. (Chinese? The thought vanished.)

They were breathing a little more heavily, but not really tired. There were no street names or numbers... they just seemed to recognize Ling Sao's oriental looking place when they got to it. Walking in they found it structured and finished exactly according to her tastes, just waiting for her to furnish it any way she desired. Looking out the window she saw many of the old *Polly Brigade* (?) wandering up and down winding little paths between flowering trees. The terrain in the area was similar to the steep hills and valleys approaching the Huangshan Mountains... Where did they know that name from? Then all of that memory seemed to rapidly fade away and she knew she was comfortably "home."

Pebbles of JADE

"Paul." It was the first time she'd called him by his given name. "I'd like to spend a little time talking with the sisters and then getting this place furnished. Then I want to quietly think about everyone I'd like to see again... and maybe finally meet a lot of folks for the *first* time. I know that will take a little time, but we have lots of that. I'll get back together with you soon. I promise. Besides, you have a lot of things to do yourself. Just remember to control your thoughts!"

She was right. They laughed, hugged again and he mentioned he would also like to do a lot of visiting. "See you around *Paradise*. Bye." Another hug... longer.

As Paul saw what had happened he began to figure this out *without* asking God... his mind was clear and sharp, as it used to be only early in the morning after a good night's rest in his previous mortal body.

Everyone, from all different parts of the old earth and from all different times in that *old earth's* history all had places prepared for them fitting their desires and former cultural expectations. Then, as their new lives on this new earth moved on, they would all develop into an interactive, world-wide community that would not only live in peaceful harmony and synchronized cooperation together with each other, but also with all of nature... especially with God, whom they were continually thanking. The whole physical universe was now available to everyone in an unlimited way. Some thoughts of the "old" earth came to him in a flash, he knew he was right-on, then just as quickly his mind faded regarding the things of old. This was breathtaking. It felt so good to *forget*. Evidently, everyone from this whole generation of human life, from Adam's seed on, was going through the same... certainly not unpleasant... experience. Except the King, he expected. Talk about how mutual experiences bond people!

"I'm going to try something out," he thought, then asked, "Lord, what should I do in my new life?" The thought came to him that he wanted to start out in a simple, but enjoyable way... and just *grow* and see what happens to lead him on. He would love to build and drive something like a Ferrari, a Maserati, or even a midget F-16. Also, he wanted powerplants available that were clean and did not consume resources... Whoa! Where did that stream of thought come from? He couldn't even remember what all that stuff was and yet he did want to be around active, interesting, beautiful people (does everyone have different taste in everything?). And why did he think of all that stuff? Then he remembered... he had just asked for guidance and clearly the King had said earlier, "His body had many parts, all with different purposes."

Suddenly, he knew where to go... and there he was in a machine/design shop ready to engage in exactly what his interests were with like-minded, really healthy and gorgeous people who could touch and interact with each other without any *fear*. Their eyes, hair, skin, stature and size... were all quite different from each other, yet all spoke in a mutually understandable tongue. No one seemed conscious of it or even wondered what language it might be... it didn't matter.

In fact, what *was* "language?" He noticed a momentary "almost" memory-moment as he asked himself if they were male or female... then it confused him a little to even think about something so strange, and the thought vanished.

He noticed a few looked as though they were pregnant and bearing little ones inside them... and he realized he would be able to do the same thing when he *wanted* to, when he was ready for the responsibility, all by himself. "Not yet," he thought, continuing, "Did I ever have any children before?" he wondered. Had he been alive before? Or, was life just beginning for him? He did not think he had always been here, but he still hadn't looked for his own home... so had he just been born? He wasn't a baby. How did he know what a baby was? It did not seem to make any difference and he found himself in a small group all touching and hugging each other, laughing softly with wet eyes. He saw others just step up to what they wanted to learn to do, and someone started showing them how. Everyone seemed patient and appreciative of what (and how) others were doing... very encouraging! One of the group mentioned that maybe they should get some coveralls... it might save a lot of bathing if they got into greasy work... and they all agreed it was a good idea.

Watching the operation for a while, he wondered "Had there ever been a time when it was not like this, with such rich and thorough selfless love? He felt like a little child and knew he was just now becoming conscious... This "living" was going to be really fun.

Ling Sao had changed her mind, out of curiosity, followed him and was standing next to him and seemed to read his mind saying, "I feel the same way. I love it... gives me goose-bumps."

Paul had been lost in thought... and jumped a little as he looked at her. "How come I can't see any?" Paul shot back and those around them all laughed.

The Sao looked at him seriously and said, "First of all, some of us former *sisters* just met outside our little homes and decided we would divide up the really young ones to live with us for a while until they are fully grown. We have also learned many people choose to live together for a variety of reasons for as long as that is their desire. But mostly I wanted to catch up with you again because... Remember just a little while ago when God told us that once before we were divided *male* and *female*... but not anymore?"

"Yes... why?"

"Well, I remembered the moment while I was talking to the others in the Polly Brigade and thought I should tell you about what I didn't mention at the time it happened... when I was with you. I was thinking about it again after you left and asked Father why."

"And... what did he say?"

"He simply explained it was to have babies, of course!" She chuckled with a husky voice that sounded familiar. "He was actually laughing! Then our Father said, 'try ***this***, and when you want to have a child, just let me know... and you will, bearing it inside you until it is physically grown strong enough to survive outside your body. Want to try it?' And I did. When I asked a few minutes ago why I was reminded of that moment when I was with you before, he told me to ask *you* to try it... said you need it."

"Try what?"

Again she was giggling, "Just think about what it was that made males and females different. God is allowing us to remember how Adam, in the original Garden of Eden, was split into two people, himself and Eve, because he was lonesome... and communication with God and the rest of nature just was not sufficient. The solution was simple for God. After the division, to become *whole* again they had to come together physically in order to reproduce another human."

"So? They already saw what the animals did."

"But these new humans were not mortal plants or animals that would always be coming and going in the natural cycle of life in nature. We were made in the image of God to be infinite and eternal. They were different, had infinitely more potential. And now, because we have multiplied so much and there are so many of us, we are no longer going to be lonesome, as Adam was...

"Pretend you're Adam... and you've not yet thought about reproducing, but you're lonely. Then you wake up from a nap and there is another human next to you whom you must join with to reproduce more humans. Just imagine what senses were triggered in both of them as they figured out what must be done in the process... but, **don't** *want* a child **yet!**" She smiled and her eyes twinkled as she watched him.

Silence.

"Go on, try… it's okay!"

"I've been working hard to control my thoughts… because of the effects. Here goes…"

Perspiration started to appear on Paul's forehead, his body convulsed and quivered, his eyes closed and his hands clenched, he tried to get his breath, and he felt near collapse. "Oh God!" he said with a wavering voice. "What was that? I don't *ever* recall having that happen inside me. That felt *so* good… it was wonderful! I feel drained and weak… Can we always do that?"

"I'm told it is available whenever we feel the need or desire."

"Oh, God! Oh, God," Paul said prayerfully, his eyes still closed. "Thank you!"

"And Voodoo-san… Isn't it curious that we can continue to remember names? Anyway, I'm told this is just the beginning! All of our heightened sensory systems technically have *no* limits! Evidently our new bodies and minds can now handle it, so we *can* experience infinitely more pleasure in everything we experiment with. It is the way He *originally* intended for humans to learn and grow in our bodies and capabilities… one step at a time.

Let's go find the others we know… *all of them!* We have so much to talk about. Our interaction with all of God's people from throughout history is now God's replacement for the *second* tree in the garden made for Adam and Eve as a little Paradise in the midst of the world that Satan had been banished to. We all will stimulate questions and clarifications from each other under God's tutorage… and from now on *we* "determine" nothing, only develop what is *good*, because God will always be in our midst.

* * *

Elona Li returned, pulled the whole group she formerly knew as the *Jades* together, and soon explained to them all about *"her"* real name… and that throughout human history *she*, as known to humans at Jade West, had served the only true Lord… who made her. The real name actually *did* translate to "Jade"… the angel. Jade was the name of a stone fitting the personal characteristics and attributes *she* had been endowed with… angels had personalities too. Jade was really just one of the many millions of God's messengers or ministers, depending on the need. *She* was permanently teamed with those who would be identified as *her* parents, but always with *different* duties, *she* was sent to protect the family at Jade West during the ultimate events before the end of time for humans… even though that was unknown at the time. They were never told exactly when that final visitation of the Creator would occur. *She* spoke with an authoritative voice that was not altogether unfamiliar.

"I have served and interacted with many humans throughout the *Generation* of Adam. The *Angel* Jade was never revealed into human history, and we servants of YHWH were never allowed to enter into or *possess* humans… even though we are entirely, what you would call, *spirit* beings. You humans are both physical and spiritual beings. The spiritual space in mankind was

BenOHADI

reserved for only the Holy Spirit of God to work in... but the corrupted nature of mankind allowed the fallen angels, demons, to trespass.

"Sometimes, I was sent to work with groups, such as when we protected the Havasupai tribe living in the Grand Canyon, who were believers in God's Christ, from evil angels around their village and especially from the evil minds of visitors that came later on. More often my duty was with individuals... many ordinary, but cherished children of the true God. A couple of the many names you would recognize from your era might be C.S. Lewis and Alexander Solzhenitsyn. Many that I ministered to were actually *rescued* by God outsmarting Lucifer such as the second Martin Luther King, Abraham Lincoln, and Thomas More... born in the year of our Lord 1478, according to the calendar you used. Perhaps some of you never learned of him. Early on after the dominion of the Christ began we were with many young families and their children. Soon I was with Monica and her son Augustine, while our little team was temporarily separated and my partners were with John Chrysostom. Before that we were also with Joseph, son of Jacob, and his family in Egypt. Our God has kept us very busy... but that is what we were created for. We cannot be everywhere at once and we certainly do not know everything. Nevertheless, we have served our Creator faithfully and many thousands of your fellow humans.

"Some other people you should know of whom we watched over, who turned out to be very important to all of you... Peter Benjamin and Su-mei Wong's

Pebbles of JADE

parents in China, all of them were under our care at different times in their lives. They prayed so often for all like you caught in your situation. In fact, we were instrumental in those two getting together to ultimately be spiritual mentors for all of you. None of them ever saw us. Did you think your identity with *Jade* was an accident?" she laughed. "There never have been any 'accidents' regarding anything. You have much to be thankful for."

For a moment their minds remembered some old things, they understood, then their minds cleared again as the Angel Jade continued.

"Unlike humans, I was not created *female*, but simply a spirit-*being* made to serve God, not reproduce. As your minds adjust to the magnitude of the spirit lives you also now can fully experience, you will come to know us as we really are, not in the guise of humans... as you now see me. However, you have now been remade as *complete beings unto yourselves* who *can* continue to reproduce by yourselves... you are no longer male and female. Yet, you will retain basic personalities, characteristics and attributes not contaminated by sin.

From now on, we will always know each other as we really are. And, yes, many humans from throughout history will remember me by different names. YHWH knows me as his servant. You may either remember me as Elona Li... or Jade.

* * * * * * * * * *

BenOHADI

The *House of Jade...All* of them, as they melted into the nations of God's "faithful" *New Israel*... in **Paradise**, knew they were all truly awake and abundantly alive for the first time... *finally!* Now they could and would learn what **"Love"** meant directly from the infinite God's incarnate ***WORD***.

+ + +

"Begin the Beguine"

8th Day

THE BEGINNING

In the beginning was the WORD…

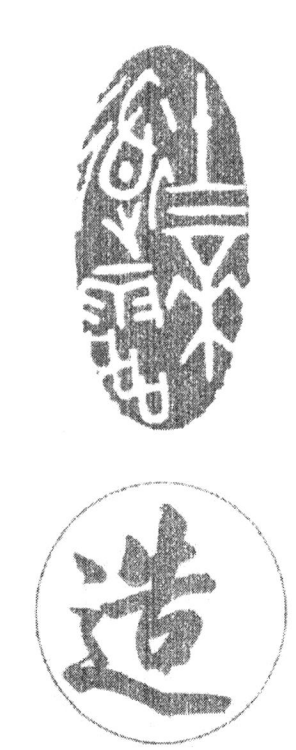

主耶穌基督，神之子，可憐我是有罪之人